# CHAMBER OF THE DRAGON PRINCE

ROYAL DRAGONS
BOOK THREE

SELINA COFFEY

LOVY BOOKS

Lovy Books Ltd
20-22 Wedlock Road
London N1 7GU
United Kingdom.

Cover by SC Creative

*A*leric, dragon prince, my fated mate, and the man I could not give in to—no matter how much I might want to—turned to add more logs to the wood-stove in the corner.

I needed a doughnut. One of those chocolate glazed creations with chocolate cream in the middle that would probably add more weight to my hips than the whole thing weighed to begin with. And a nice, cold shower.

With a glance out of the window, I decided maybe a cold shower wasn't a good idea. I'd never get warm again if I did that. The doughnut sounded like a good idea though.

I wasn't sure these were the normal thoughts of a woman who'd recently been kidnapped, but it wasn't like Aleric was a stranger to me. He was my mate. My dragon mate, and he knew my secret. One of them, anyway.

"What do you really think you're going to accomplish with this, Aleric?" I groused at him, not in a good mood at all. Not even the sultry tilt of his eyelids could help my mood. He'd kidnapped me from my family—shifted and swooped off with me as our kin celebrated the birth of our newest family member. Both of our families, his family and mine.

"Well, you always avoid me, Edana, or you only want to meet in places filled with people. You're too busy, life is in the way; you have work, family obligations… an entire list of reasons why you can't spend time with me. There are none of those things here. There is only us and the wind." He turned back to the fire and poked at it until the flames roared high.

"And a shit-ton of snow," I mumbled as I looked out at the darkness. Had I really slept for more than eight hours as he'd said I did when I first woke up? I didn't believe it. I hadn't slept for more than five hours since I was eighteen-years-old.

"Pardon?" he asked in that delicious mixture of an Irish and English accent.

"Nothing. I guess it's fortunate I can't fly away then." That wasn't an easy thing to say in normal times. It was even more stressful right now.

"It is unfortunate that you didn't get the ability with

your dragon side." He hid a small smile, and I wanted to kick him for his impertinence. Instead, I sat down on the ratty old couch and huffed. He didn't mean it as an insult at least. I wouldn't know how to respond to that at all. "But in this weather, even with dragon skills, you'd not get far. Plus, there's your fear of heights."

I glanced back at him again. How did he know about that? I'd never told anyone that. Deep down, I thought it was why I couldn't shift. If I shifted I had to fly, and flight meant being up in the air where I didn't want to be. Instead of denying it, I changed the subject.

"My employers will look for me, my family..." I began but stopped when he turned to me with a serious expression. Something about the pensive twist to his lips said I wouldn't like what he had to say. I braced myself and tilted an eyebrow up as I waited.

"I'm sure they will, but why would they look here?" He was an extremely logical man, for a poet.

I let my inquisitive look turn sour as he stood up and wiped his hands on a wet towel. "Well, what do you want to eat?"

"Excuse me?" That was a new direction I hadn't expected.

"You haven't eaten in at least twelve hours, surely you're hungry?" he asked as he headed for the door. He walked out and quickly came back in with a bag of food.

"There's a fridge out there. No power, of course, but in this cold it's not needed. What do you want?"

He offered me a selection of chicken, beef, or shrimp. I chose the beef and hoped he was going to make a soup out of it. The cold had started to settle into my bones while I was outside, and I still hadn't shaken it.

He went about cutting up vegetables and the meat, using a bowl and hot water from a pot on the wood stove to wash up with. He put a pot on the other side and started the meat. Then he added vegetables, some fresh herbs, and a few spices. By the time it was simmering my stomach growled. In another pot, he whipped up an omelet.

"Just to tide you over until the soup is done." It was like he'd read my mind.

I squinted and wondered if he had. From what I'd read, it was possible between true mates.

I didn't want to think about it, so I concentrated until I knew my defenses were all up and in place, and settled back on the couch. I looked around the large, open room more closely. There really was no need for a kitchen, if you were cooking on the stove and didn't have a sink anyway. The pots and pans Aleric used looked new, so he must have bought those on his shopping expedition. I glanced around and saw a set of dishes and tableware on a shelf at the other end of the room.

Blankets were stacked up on that shelf too, along with dry and canned food, a few different kinds of juice, water, and wine. I saw clothes on another shelf—for both men and women—and coats, gloves, and hats hung on pegs by the door. All in all, he'd done what he could to make this home. Reality set in.

He really meant for this to be our home for whatever amount of time he'd chosen. He wasn't planning on taking me home anytime soon. As he'd said, the place was remote; I couldn't actually escape anywhere. The temperature made it far too dangerous to try to go outside. For all intents and purposes, I was his prisoner.

So why didn't that terrify me? Why did I feel a little thrill go up my spine and straight down between my thighs? It was more than my training, the experience my work had given me. It was Aleric. The man fascinated me, he haunted my dreams, and I wanted him.

I'd never been able to deny the fact, but I'd struggled and fought hard to resist. I didn't have time for a mate. My work was far more important. More important than the kind of love Malcolm and Arista had found. Those two had been through hell and back, and I could still barely believe his own father had imprisoned him for falling in love with her.

You couldn't help who your mate turned out to be. You could fight it, yeah, but eventually you'd die from it. Which meant I didn't plan to fight my own self for very long. I would for however long I could, though. I knew there was no talking him out of this, at least not right now, so I settled back on the couch and scanned the titles of the books on the flimsy coffee table in front of me.

Arista had been taken to a cave, but eventually to nice hotels, palaces, even a villa that wasn't exactly luxurious, but at least it was warm. Willow had been taken all over the world, the best hotels, a prince's home, an Amazunian village, and then to a wonderful home Henry bought for her. Aleric brought me to a cabin on a frozen mountaintop.

I couldn't decide whether he was a sadistic shit or if he might be the smartest man in the world. He'd out maneuvered me well. I had to give him credit for that.

"Here. Sorry there's no toast, I crushed the bread on the way up here." He looked sheepish about that, but I couldn't help but grin.

"Not everything going to plan then?" I taunted him, and he took it in stride.

"No, but it will. Eventually." He gave me a mysterious smile that made my heart thump in my chest.

Damn. What did he mean by that?

I ate the omelet in silence, picked up a book, and flipped through the pages as we waited for the soup to cook. It was so quiet, even with the fire, that I could hear fresh snow falling outside. Thanks a lot, Mother

Nature, way to work against me. Dump more of the stuff on me!

Wind blasted against the front door, as if a mythical being answered me, and I frowned. Coincidence, nothing more.

I pretended to read the book while he puttered around. He opened cabinets to find them empty or full of even older books in a language I couldn't speak. He opened metal coffee cans with plastic lids and found papers, some old currency that I also didn't recognize, assorted nut and bolts. I continued to turn pages, but I didn't read a word; my eyes were on every single move Aleric made.

Escape was impossible, for now, so I'd settle in. I knew my boss wouldn't find me up here and that mayhem would ensue, but there was little I could do about it. Aleric wasn't about to budge. My family might notice I'd left, but they'd assume I was with Aleric; which would be correct, or that I'd gone back to my life.

There was little I could do but try to resist the coming onslaught to my senses and try to make the best of the situation. He was attractive after all, and could be funny. He was a kind soul, but there was also that dragon band of steel in his backbone that I couldn't resist. Even this whole kidnap situation was poetic but forceful.

What maiden didn't dream of being swept away by a

handsome devil bent on twisting her into knots of pleasure? He hadn't made one single advance though, not since I'd kissed him and then backed off. He knew it was best to let me pace it out, and that's what he'd done so far. Even if he was the one pacing as he waited for our food to cook.

"You might as well sit down. That soup is going to take a while." I pointed at the end of the couch. It really was gross. I don't know if you could call the wool cloth that covered it a single color; it seemed to be woven strands of a variety of colors that got thrown into the heading of "autumn" back in the 1970s and never quite left it. I just knew it was itchy and gross. Even if it was comfortable to lie on.

"Ahem. Well, I think I'll check the bathroom again. I might have missed something." His lips twisted as he moved away, and I wondered what had upset him.

"What are you looking for?"

"Nothing, just seeing what's here. It's like a treasure trove of a former life." There's the poet again.

I felt my lips twitch into a smile, and I stretched my legs out on the couch. If he wasn't about to sit down, I might as well.

"That's the cutest thing I've heard since I heard Marya cry earlier today."

He humphed in reply, and my smile turned into a grin.

I wasn't the most beautiful woman on earth, I had my faults such as hips that were too wide no matter how often I run, but I wasn't bad to look at. I had long black hair that hung around my hips when I let it down, which wasn't often, and gray eyes that more than one man had complimented. Aleric most of all. He loved my eyes; the windows to my soul, as he said.

He was far more stunning than me. Tall, with blond hair and blue eyes, he had the body of a warrior but the soul of a much gentler man. He was worth a million photos, then some, this man who wanted me so desperately he'd kidnapped me.

I wondered if he'd want sex after dinner. I knew I wouldn't be able to resist long, not without an excuse to walk away. Here, I couldn't tell him I had to get back to work, or that Willow needed me, or that I had an appointment. There was no way I could hold him off and that worried me.

I didn't want to have sex with him because our natures drove us to it. I wanted it to be because we wanted to. When I had the time to devote to him and nothing but him. I'd seen how Willow and Arista changed after they mated with their dragons. The world stopped existing for them. There was nothing outside of their desire for their mate, and now their children.

I didn't have that luxury. I had responsibilities that went far beyond anything they had to cope with. My job was special; I'd been chosen out of a few, and then trained to be the best out of those few. There was no one else who could do the tasks I'd been given. Aleric put far more than my world in danger with this little stunt, even if he didn't know. Both of our worlds depended on me, and right now, he'd put that all in danger.

My boss would oversee things for a while, but he couldn't keep it up for long. Eventually, he'd either have to find me or replace me. But we all knew I was the best at my job. There were only a few half-shifters left in my world. There was a reason for that. We could be very dangerous weapons, in the wrong hands and with improper training.

I'd been found early, when I needed a new direction the most. Since then, I'd devoted my life to my mission. I'd done everything in my power to make sure that human and shifter world did not collide. Aleric had endangered all of that with this stunt.

But when he came back in, face full of curiosity over some dusty box he'd found in the bedroom, I couldn't make him take me home. He wouldn't anyway, but if I asked, he might. Maybe. A day or two, surely I could hold out, just for a day or two.

"What did you find?" I asked, the dim twinkle of a ruby caught my eye. "What the hell?"

"I'm guessing it's a jewelry box, but I don't know. I

can't open it." He handed the box to me, and we both jumped when we heard a click and the top popped open.

"What did you do?" he asked as he sat down beside me.

"Nothing. It just opened." We both looked inside, a single piece of thick paper a mystery that might keep me curious enough to stay here. I pulled the paper out and looked at it. It was an old scroll, and the leather straps that kept it rolled up crumbled as I touched them. What was this?

2

———

"What is it?" Aleric asked and leaned over to look at the paper.

"I don't know, I can't tell…" I trailed off as the letters danced before my eyes but didn't solidify into anything that made sense.

"That's a dragon scroll," Aleric said with certainty and picked it up from my lap.

"What does it say?" I asked and leaned toward him.

"I'm not sure. Since the box opened for you, I'm sure it must be meant for you and not me." He gave me the paper back and went to check the soup.

It didn't matter how I turned the paper or how I looked at it, I couldn't make it make sense. The words just kept… running away was the only way I could put it. "Come on, put it away for now. We'll figure it out later. Right now, you need to eat, then we'll get some sleep. It's going to be a long day tomorrow, and this wood won't last. We'll have to cut more."

I wanted to glare at him and tell him I was an adult and could do as I pleased, but didn't. I was tired again, and I knew that even with the fire going it was going to just get colder as the night went on. That's why I didn't protest when he followed me to the bed after we finished eating and cleaned out the bowls. He put the pot of soup on a small table in the corner. It would cool and probably be icy by the time we got up.

I wasn't exactly excited to crawl into bed with him after I washed up for the night. Well I was, but I didn't want to be. I wanted to sleep and suspected it would take me hours. Instead, it took moments. I woke up a couple of times like when Aleric got up to add more wood to the fire, but otherwise I slept even better than I had earlier.

When I woke up to find the world still dark, I wasn't surprised. I got up, pottered around until I found the items my mom used to use to make coffee with, and started a pot. When that was on its way, I started to heat bread on a flat griddle. I hoped it would turn out like toast. Afterward, even if it did take forever and a day, I set the bread aside and started on the eggs and a pack of bacon I'd found in the fridge. I found it outside, around the back where the wood was stacked up.

I noted there wasn't much left, and knew how he planned to spend the day.

I wasn't afraid of hard work, I already had my boots on and had breakfast ready, didn't I? I sipped at coffee, the eggs and bacon on a plate beside the toast, and looked out at the world as the sun came up. The window was small, but I could see out of it.

There wasn't much around us but more snow and lumps that could be hills or just gigantic piles of snow. I had no way of knowing. Aleric came in then, a smile on his still sleepy face.

"Good morning," he mumbled with a sheepish grin. His hair stuck up in fifty directions, his eyes were still droopy, and he had a five o'clock shadow. He hadn't brushed his teeth or anything yet, and the thermal pajama pants he had on were slung low around his waist. Something deep inside of me screamed *want*.

I told it to shut up and went to stack a plate with food for him. I let him handle his coffee, and stacked a plate for myself.

"How did you make toast?" he mumbled as he shuffled to the couch and sat his plate down, coffee beside of it.

"Hillbilly ingenuity, my dear fellow," I said with a grin. I'd already brushed my hair, cleaned up, and was ready for breakfast when I sat down beside him.

"Seriously? In case I wake up before you one morning?" His smile, perfectly straight teeth and all, faltered.

That was a bit of a slip. That meant he planned to be here awhile. I let it go. Make the best of it for now, that's all I could do, right?

"I used the pan and kept flipping it to make sure it didn't burn. It's not the best toast in the world, but it'll work." I shrugged and stood up to clean the plates that were now empty.

I took them to the large bowl of hot water I'd prepared, and slipped the plates inside. I scrubbed them down and cleaned the pots while he watched.

"You're amazing, do you know that?" He looked like he meant it. The compliment made me uncomfortable for some reason, and I frowned down at the pot.

"This is how I grew up, Aleric. Well, it wasn't this ancient." I flapped my hand around to indicate the cabin. "But the water would freeze in the winter, the power would go out, and you had to be able to fend for yourself or die waiting on someone to come save you."

"Wow. I didn't realize."

"All of us grew up that way. Life is improving for all of us, but Arista, Willow, and I grew up just like this." I knew it was true, and it didn't bother me a bit. I knew if a disaster struck, I'd make it through. Or if a man kidnapped me and dragged me off to a remote mountain top.

"We weren't always in the lap of luxury growing up." Aleric paused, and somehow I knew he was thinking about the fact that I was six years older than him. It didn't bother me, but it might him. I wondered if it did.

At thirty-five, there was very little that could faze me anymore. "How did you grow up then?"

"Well, for a time, we lived a very simple life. I'm not sure what happened, I was only around five at the time. Father moved us all to this tiny little house without any kind of conveniences or staff to help us. That's when we learned to chop wood and cook on a stove. Even when we went back to the palace he would still make us cook or chop wood regularly, and teach us how to fend for ourselves in the woods. Things like that."

"Ah. I see." I put the now clean dishes back on the shelf. I stored the information away. For a time, they'd abandoned the castle. That wasn't something my boss knew about this family, but would when I returned.

I swiped my hair back into place and smiled. "Well, do you want to clean up and join me outside? We'll take care of that pile of wood that isn't chopped and bring some in."

He nodded, and I finished dressing to go outside. He'd bought extreme-weather gear for us both, and I barely felt the cold as I stepped out. Except in the areas that were exposed to the cold. I swore my bottom lip was frozen by the time he came out to see I had already started on the wood.

"You're left-handed," he noted with a smile. "So am I."

"How can you tell?" I looked at him closely; this was an odd observation to make while chopping wood.

"The way you swing. You do it left-handed." He demonstrated by splitting some wood himself.

"And how do other people do it then?" I asked, not seeing his point. He changed hands and in an instant, I understood. "Huh. I never knew there was a difference."

"Yep, there is. Shall I take over?"

"Be my guest," I said, and started to stack wood in my arms to take inside.

In two hours all of the wood was chopped, stacked, and plenty of it was in the house.

"There's more under a pile of snow, but I thought we'd save that for hard times," he said quietly, a twinge of guilt on his face that he quickly smoothed away.

"Good, idea. I'll make coffee, you make more heat." I wiggled my eyebrows at him flirtatiously, and he grinned.

"Don't tease. It's too cold. I need all of the blood in my body to stay where it's at." He gave me a cocky grin that made my heart flutter.

"I bet you do." I wanted to add a smirk and a 'big boy', but controlled myself. For some reason, that grin just made me want to crawl all over him and shift his blood down to that one area for him.

I'd decided to play along, for now. It was all I could do, wasn't it? It wasn't like I could just get up and walk out to the street and scream for help. Or call someone. I couldn't get a signal from my psychic cousins, mainly because I'd closed my mind off to such things a long time ago. Arista would be capable of it, if I'd let her. But I held back. Even a moment of letting down that trap around my brain could be disastrous, especially if my mate could read my mind.

I watched him as he went back to feeding wood into the stove. It took a lot to keep even this tiny cabin warm, and I knew we'd run out eventually. Perhaps that would be the moment I could escape. Unless Aleric found a way to bring more wood up to the cabin to keep us warm.

If I was totally honest with myself, the fact that he'd kidnapped me didn't bother me at all. I felt the need to be with him, even when I was busy with work. I thought about him, dreamed about him, and to be with him was a pleasure, really. It was like that moment when a spot that had itched until it drove you mad was finally scratched. Pure relief and bliss.

*Why not enjoy the time I had with him, instead of playing it so angry,* I pondered while the coffee simmered on the stove. I watched it to make sure it didn't boil, that would spoil the taste, but my thoughts distracted me. *Why not enjoy the time,* one side of my brain said quietly? The other said, *you know why.*

I did know why, he would totally consume me. I'd be able to function properly eventually, but for those first few months, maybe even years, he'd be my focus and everything else. Well, it just wouldn't matter so much. In my line of work, that could be deadly.

He'd asked me a dozen times what I did for a living, but I'd always avoided a straight answer. It was a secret, one that couldn't be revealed. I had so many of them, I was almost certain I was made entirely of them, every single strand of my DNA. My secrets kept my family, and the world, safe.

A vibration from the metal pot caught my attention, and I pulled it away with a towel. I'd almost ruined the coffee. Time to pay attention again. I caught a glimpse of the box with the paper in it and wondered about the paper once more. It was obviously magical, and I had to guess it had decided I was the one who should read it, because the box had opened for me without a struggle.

I picked it up after we'd both settled down on the couch with a cup of coffee. What did it say? I took the paper out of the box again, but the letters just glowed and shifted around, not letters at all. Sometimes I'd catch a glimpse of one that would almost make sense, but then it would become something else before I could be certain. Was that a 'w' or an 'm' that was upside down? Then it was gone, a shape of lines and curves that made no sense at all.

I sighed and put it back in the box. I'd try again some other time.

"So, Aleric, what are we supposed to do to pass the time in this secluded cabin?" I asked in a bright voice, my eyes on his dark-lashed ones. They were such beautiful eyes, I could drown in them. "It's too cold to go outside for a walk, and honestly, fuck that idea. Chopping wood is enough time out there for me."

"Well, what do you like to do when you're at home?" His hand came out to mine, and I felt heat travel up my fingers and through my arm where he'd touched me. I pulled my hand away and glared at him. I wanted to tell him not to touch me, it distracted me, but knew he'd pounce on that admission. Besides, he'd mentioned home, where I didn't have to look for something to do, because there was always something at hand.

"Watch movies, listen to music while I read, run on my treadmill, knit blankets that aren't exactly the right shape from patterns I've found online. You know, things modern humans do."

He had the sense to swallow guiltily and pulled his hand back to brush his golden hair away from his face. "Oh."

"Yes. Oh. I might have grown up like this, but there

was always something to do. Coloring books, books to read, playing cards, something that needed to be repaired." That was, until my Mom passed away and I was left with my father. But then, he'd left too, and I'd been alone.

None of that was worth my time to think about. It was in the past, long gone and buried in more ways than one. "So any ideas besides the obvious?"

"Well, I could go down and see if I can find something in the town…" Aleric's words trailed off. For obvious reasons he didn't want me to think about that town.

"Or," I stretched the word out before I continued. "You could take me home."

I said that last part without emphasis, just matter of fact and sensible. Aleric looked away. "I'll go find something in town. I'll be back shortly."

I sighed and sat back against the armrest of the terrible couch. I wanted to go home. I wanted to take him to bed and create our own special kind of heat. I couldn't do either of those. So instead, I wandered about the cabin while I waited.

I felt like a caged animal.

## 3

———

 $\mathcal{I}$ might just be crazy. After a week of snow, wind, and Aleric so near to me, I might just be crazy. I couldn't sleep and turned from my side to my back in the bed. I crammed my hands down beside me in tight fists and sighed deeply. I would not touch him, I would not!

My pinkie poked out and stroked at the side of his hand beside of mine.

I rolled my eyes behind closed eyelids at my body's betrayal. His heat was such a temptation. I could feel it, even when I didn't touch him. It would be so easy to roll over, throw my arm over him and take some of that warmth. Even with the fire, some nights were still cold, and tonight was bitter.

I flopped over to my side, away from him, and stared into the darkness. I wanted more than just a cuddle.

That was the real problem. If Aleric was an ordinary man, I could fuck him and move on. Or cuddle him and move on. He was my mate, and I wanted him so much. His silky warmth was a temptation I could no longer resist, not in those dark, cold hours of the night.

I let my hand wander under the covers, three blankets and a thick quilt, almost too heavy to move under, and tentatively placed my hand just above his hip. Silky smooth skin delighted my fingers until they softly curled into his flesh. He felt so good.

I held my breath, afraid to wake him up, because if he woke up and looked at me with that same desire that was always in his eyes, I knew I wouldn't be able to resist anymore. His breath remained even, unchanged, and my touch grew bolder. I slid my hand down across his lower abdomen, along the edge of his pajama pants, my pinkie just curling under the cloth. It was probably wrong, I probably shouldn't have touched him like this, but I wanted to know what he felt like.

A human woman would have already given into Aleric's allure, she would already be his. I was half dragon, half slayer; I was made of stronger stuff, but... but. He was my mate.

I went still when his hips moved into my touch, and he made a sound. My name? Heat curled between my thighs, muscles deep within clenched as I let it all wash over me.

"I can smell your need, Edana. Let me make the ache go away."

I went totally still, I didn't even breathe. My pinky was still just under his pants, and all I'd have to do was slide my hand lower.

"Why do you continue to resist, woman? It will only grow worse until you start to become sick. You need this as much as I do." He moved and abruptly my hand went from the edge of his pants to the long, thick ridge below. I cupped him instinctively and inhaled sharply. He felt so hot, so hard. My fingers twitched, and he groaned in response.

I would only touch him for a moment, I told myself, just a moment, just to satisfy my curiosity. Only long enough to wring another one of those gut-wrenching groans out of him. But I couldn't stop. My hand continued to slide up and down his shaft through the soft cotton of his pants. His sounds, those soft sounds of delight, of his need for more, drove me on.

He was helpless in this moment, and a scent came to me that made something deep inside me tremble. It was intoxicating, that smell, and somehow, I knew it was the smell of Aleric's desire. Subtle spices and mint, maybe even rosemary, but something more that heightened my desire. I bent forward, until I found his lips with mine, at last.

Desire had already flared, but now it became a fierce

fire that almost consumed us. My hand gripped him tighter, until he hissed and moaned at the same time. His head fell back, and I felt his passion as my own. I felt his pleasure as a sensation within my own body, and when he grasped at my breast, I was shocked to feel the world explode.

It was quick, fierce, and unexpected, but it shook me to my core. His lips came back to mine, and I felt a pulse travel through his hardened length. My mate followed me into a fire that did not burn, not the normal black world I was used to. I'd experienced the pleasure of sex and orgasms before, but nothing prepared me for the way our dragons intertwined, even if mine was weaker. After all, I could not shift, but in that moment, the orange and blue flames of our dragons merged into a silver flame unlike anything I'd ever seen before. The world became colors behind my closed eyelids, and pleasure was all I knew. Aleric was all I knew.

We shivered together as we came back to reality, but not from the cold. I looked into his eyes, little more than a sparkle in the darkness, and saw a flame I knew was a reflection from mine. It wasn't full consummation but our souls had merged, our dragons had merged, and now we would never be able to part. For a few hours perhaps, maybe a day or two, but if we tried to stay apart any longer than that, we'd start to die.

Before, we could have spent days and weeks apart,

maybe even months, but now, we'd start to feel tired within hours. I kissed him and turned away, my mind a mess. He was in my soul now, a part of me, and I felt him there, as though he embraced me. I stared into the darkness, unsure of whether I actually liked the fact I was no longer alone.

There was nothing I could do about it now. That sensation would only grow stronger, not weaker, as time passed by. We were now one, whether I liked it or not. It was my own fault, Aleric hadn't forced this on me, I could have gone on with my resistance, but I'd wanted to know what he felt like. I couldn't regret the moment, I just needed time to adjust.

"Are you alright, Edana?" he asked quietly, his voice a reassurance in the darkness. His hand came down to my hip, a gesture of comfort.

"Yes. I just need to… adjust." I'd been on my own for a very long time. Even my previous sexual encounters had been about physical gratification, not a need for company. This was totally different.

Another soul had fused to mine, and I had a lot of secrets to keep. From him, from the world. I wasn't sure I'd be able to protect all of that now.

"I wouldn't do anything to harm you, Edana, ever. I have had a hard time maintaining my loyalty to my father lately. He has done some things I cannot agree with at all. The fact he's an addict doesn't help. He nearly killed Malcolm and Arista. Willow and Henry didn't have it much better, and now they're both banished. The things he's done, the things he's hidden. You'll know it all soon. So you'll also know that my loyalty lies with you now, not anyone or anything else. Your secrets are safe, my darling."

I squeezed his hand, still on my hip, and gave a weak smile in the darkness. I felt a warmth around my heart and grimaced a little. Fuck. The warm and fuzzies! I thought I'd hardened myself against those kinds of feelings. Over the many days I'd known Aleric now, and the most recent ones with constant contact, I'd had to admit that I didn't just have a mate; I had a man I'd come to love.

I turned back to him, and he took me in his arms. There weren't many words I wanted to say, so I just settled beneath his chin and let the wind howling outside sing me back to sleep. I dreamed of his childhood, and things that barely made any sense, but when did dreams ever really make sense?

WHEN I WOKE up and finished my morning ritual, he had the coffee on, had heated water for some oatmeal, and had it all on the coffee table in front of the couch. I sat down, unsure of how to approach him. I was normally in control, I always knew what to do. Believe it or not, I'd never had the morning after conversation. I'd made it clear they were to leave afterward, and they always had. Aleric was the first man I'd ever woken up with.

I smiled when he smiled, and then I leaned over, my fingers on the buttons of his flannel shirt. "Hi."

"Hi, babe," he replied, and leaned down to kiss me. I pulled him closer, deepened the kiss, until I shivered when his tongue slicked over mine. God, he tasted so good.

"Coffee's getting cold." He pulled away and I sputtered, but he just ignored me. I could have sworn for a moment he smirked, but the corners of his mouth fell back into place and his face was serene when he handed me a hot mug of coffee.

"Great, thanks." What was this? I thought he'd want to take me straight back to bed, to pin me to the couch and rip my pajama bottoms away so that he could get between my thighs unhampered. Instead, he slid my bowl of oatmeal closer and poured hot water into it.

We were in silence, and I felt amused fury heat my cheeks up. The fucker. He'd just turned the tables on me!

He was the one playing hard to get now! I'd finally given in to my own body's needs, and now he wanted to use that against me. Two could play that game. I took my bowl and ate my peaches and cream oatmeal without complaint. When I was finished, I stuck the spoon in my mouth and licked it rather thoroughly. My action caught his eye, but he only looked at me with amusement before he took the bowl and the spoon and washed them with the rest of the dishes.

Hmmm. I went into the bathroom, let down my hair from the braid I'd plaited it into, and brushed out the dark length. I opened a few of the buttons on my flannel shirt and looked at myself. I could get by without makeup, and usually did, so I didn't worry about that. It was the game I was about to play that worried me. Would we crack more than our wills with this game we'd decided on?

I wasn't sure, but now that I'd had a taste of that low sound he made when he'd come, a sound that went all the way through me, I wanted more. I had visions of being on my knees in front of the couch, his hand buried in my hair. Other images flashed around behind my closed eyelids; Aleric beneath me on the bed, with me bent over the back of the couch, pinned to the door as he held me up to take every inch he had to give me.

I felt a tremble of need shake me and knew I had to win this game somehow. I wanted him to take me, but I also wanted to take him. It was a race to see who would win. The good news was, either way, we both came out the winners.

He ruined it all when I came out of the bathroom, ready to seduce.

"I need to get a few things. I'll be back in a few hours."

"What?" I asked and felt my face frown in confusion. "You're leaving me here?"

"It's only for a little while," he promised and came up to cup my face with his right hand.

I tilted my head to look up at him. "But I don't want you to go." I tried to hold him tight so he wouldn't leave, but he only dropped a kiss on my nose and pulled away.

"I won't be long," he promised.

He went to the door and hesitated. He was coming back, my heart sang. Well, it wasn't really my heart, it was something lower, but then I forgot to think because he stole my thoughts when he pulled me up and leaned me into the wall to kiss me. My legs happily wrapped around his waist, and I thought I'd won as his tongue danced with mine and his hands kneaded my ass. Oh, he was mine now.

Then he set me down, walked out, and flew away. He hadn't even taken the time to shut the door. *Stubborn bastard knew if he waited another second he'd lose,* I thought with a smirk as I closed the door. Okay, so maybe my legs wobbled a little, a lot, and my heart raced in my chest. I would bring him to his knees one way or another.

If he was going to be gone for hours, I'd use the time wisely. I went about filling every pot I could with snow, and then put those on the stove to melt and boil. I spent the first hour filling the tub with water. I'd gone through the supplies Aleric had brought up, found everything I needed, and spent some time in the hot depths of the oddly-shaped tub. It wasn't very long, but it was deep, and I was able to make sure every part of my body that mattered was smooth and ready for his touch.

When I got out, I dried my hair into a halo braid by the fire. I wasn't looking to win a contest for hairstyle of the year, I just wanted to look soft and feminine when he got back. I found a clean pair of pajamas, a silky set hidden in the bottom of a bag I hadn't checked yet. They were silk, a shimmery shade that matched my eyes exactly. The spaghetti straps and thin material would mean I was cold, but I put on the thick robe he'd brought me and that kept the cold at bay, even with the tie undone.

I put the pots away and waited. Let battle commence.

4

When Aleric came back, I was asleep. There wasn't a lot for a girl to do on her own, and I'd read all of the books and magazines he'd brought me. When I woke up, he had several bags packed and had them all tied together.

"What's going on?" I asked and sat up.

"Get dressed, we're going in a few minutes." He didn't say much more than that, and he didn't seem agitated, so I sat there and blinked at him.

"Going where?" I asked, finally.

"Somewhere warm. You'll need your thermal coat and pants for a while. Come on, let's get out of this cold."

"But..." I started. He looked at me in question. "I kind of like the cold."

"I promise you'll like where we're going much better."

I watched him and waited, but he didn't say anything else. I kind of wanted him to say we were going back to civilization, that we'd have a nice room in a resort with electricity, but he didn't.

I dressed, put on my coat and boots, and climbed on board when he shifted. Aleric always shifted into a black dragon; sometimes he had red accents, sometimes blue. He could change sizes too. Right now, he was big enough that I could sit between his shoulder blades and not feel the wind. It was a natural recess and I didn't have to worry about falling off unless he turned over, so I watched the sky around me change as we passed through clouds.

I watched for a while, hoping to see something familiar, but nothing appeared because we were too high. I didn't even know if we were still in my world. We could even be in a totally different world from either of ours.

I didn't know how many parallel universes there were, but I knew there were three known ones. There were two additional ones that only my organization knew about still. Those two had hidden themselves from the world a long time ago and refused to be found, though there were still references to them in some ancient texts. I wondered if Aleric had brought the scroll in the box. I'd have checked the bags around me, but exhaustion took over and I curled up and went back to sleep.

I woke up again when Aleric landed. Here the sun was down, but I felt a warm breeze when he sat me down on the ground. Tropical flowers scented the air, and I heard the sound of rushing surf. An island?

"Hawaii?" I asked, delighted to feel warm air again. I stripped off the coat, my flannel shirt, and then decided to go all the way and stripped down to my bra and panties.

"It's not Hawaii, but something like it. There's no hotels or bars, just a small house with a bed and a generator for the air conditioner, appliances, and the lights."

I wasn't disappointed there wasn't a television. The fact there was a fridge and lights suited me. I looked behind me and saw the beach was just there. I laughed with delight and finished stripping down. When I plunged into the waves, I was totally naked and didn't care. I was warm, and the world wasn't frozen anymore!

Aleric sat on the beach for a moment and watched, but then he carried the rest of the bags down to the house further down the small island's beach. I could see the place wasn't very big, the island or the house, but it was enough. I knew I'd have to get back to work soon, but I wanted to enjoy this place for a little while.

I hadn't had a real vacation... ever. I'd gone on

overnight trips, usually for work, and I'd traveled a lot, but it was always work related when I took the long trips.

I swam in the surf for a little while longer, and by the time I got out, dripping wet but awake at last, Aleric had the lights on and had opened the windows and doors. There were a lot of windows, most of the walls were designed to open up to let in the tropical breeze, and there were doors to four other rooms.

"Hey. This is the living room, obviously," he said as I walked into the open room with furniture that sat low to the floor. The views of the moonlit beach were spectacular, I had to admit. There were doors to four rooms along the other three sides. One was a bathroom with closets, a bed, and one huge window for a wall. The other was kitchen, a bathroom, and another bedroom.

"I'll take this room if you want the other?" Aleric offered, a knowing grin on his face.

"Pardon?" I asked, and turned back from the view in the room I thought we'd share.

"I thought maybe you'd want to sleep on your own for a while," he offered and walked away.

"Oh, no, you can sleep with me." I followed behind him, confused. "Really, I'd like it if you did."

"No, I think after last night we both need some time to think, don't you?" He took out a pad of paper and a pen from one of the bags and headed for the front door.

"I'm going to write for a while. There's food in the fridge if you want anything, and I won't be long. I need to clear my head a little after that flight."

"Oh. Alright." What else could I say? I'd just been thoroughly dismissed.

*Maybe this wasn't a game, after all,* I thought while I showered. Maybe Aleric was upset. That thought hadn't occurred to me at all. I was so used to men who took what they wanted and left without a backward glance. This was different, Aleric was different.

I hurried out of the shower, put on one of his t-shirts as a nightgown, and went back out into the kitchen. I chewed at my lip as I found a bottle of wine and poured myself a glass. I nibbled from a plate of cheese I'd found and went into the living room. It was a tranquil room, meant for peace while you watched the waves outside. I couldn't see much at the moment, only what the moonlight revealed, but I could see Aleric out there in the darkness.

He sat with his legs stretched out before him on the sand, his hands behind him to prop him up. He wasn't writing at all, just watching the waves. I thought, perhaps, I'd been wrong about quite a lot of things since I'd met him.

I knew what he was, and what we were to each other. I'd been so afraid of losing myself in him that I'd blocked out what he might need. I was so used to being on my own, to total independence, that I'd actually been quite selfish. I'd given Aleric as little of my time as possible; not because I hated him or didn't want him, but because I'd been afraid of what was about to happen. Maybe I'd hurt him?

I poured more of the delicious red wine into my glass and watched him on the beach. He was handsome, there was no doubt about that, and the rich timber of his voice and laughter had lodged into my memory. Everything about Aleric was beautiful, even that he was a soldier and a poet was beautiful.

I'd spent my entire life fending for myself. When my mother died, my father had fallen apart. I'd only been a child, twelve-years-old, so I didn't know exactly what had gone on, but I could remember there was a woman who used to come to the house after I'd gone to bed. I would hear their voices, but not the words they said. I still didn't know who she was, but I did know that during the day, Dad was usually passed out from too much wine and that I'd had to learn to cook to feed myself.

After a while, Dad took off without even saying goodbye. His personal items were gone, and I was in the house on my own. I'd heard whispers from others in the family. He'd been a degenerate who'd caused Mom's death; he was a drunk, and I was better off. He and my mother hadn't been mates, but they'd loved each other.

My brain was a mess at that point, and I looked away from Aleric. Perhaps I was too much like my father. Maybe he deserved better than me? Fate had deemed us mates, though, unlike my parents. I got up from the couch and pushed open the panel of glass that made up the wall. I wanted to call out to him, to bring him closer to me, so that I could smell his scent. The wind brought faint whispers of Aleric's unique smell to me, and I closed my eyes to savor it.

I'd ignored my past since I left my family all those years ago. I hadn't counted on anyone but my team members and my boss. There'd been no need to trust anyone more than them. There'd been no need to rely on anyone but myself. I needed to change that with Aleric in my life now.

He deserved to have a mate who was there for him. I couldn't be totally there for him just yet, my work was for too important for that, but I could give him more of my time than I had before. I could let him in.

"Aleric?" I called out, my hand on the pane of glass, as if to hold me inside of the house, to ground me while my mouth spoke the words that would make me take flight into an unknown world.

"What's wrong, Edana?" He stood up. His eyes gleamed in the moonlight, and I felt as if my body was slowly being drawn to him, particle by particle.

"You're right, you know? We need to spend more

time together. We need to, well…" I paused when my voice started to shake. This was a huge step for me. I was giving up some of my own autonomy, and I had never wanted to do that before. Aleric had changed all of that, he'd changed me. "You took a chance when you took me from my family. In my world, you'd deserve it if you were arrested. But I know why you did it. I know why you took that chance."

"And why is that?" His voice was patient, without accusation, only curiosity.

"Because we deserve it." That might have been the hardest admission of all.

Motherless, then fatherless, I'd never felt as if I was good enough for a family deep down inside. My grandmother had taken me in, then she had died as well when I was sixteen. I was old enough to be on my own by then, and most of the family had left me to get on with life, as was their way. I'd never been able to openly admit I'd felt worthless before, not even to myself, but now I could. I could also now admit that I deserved a lot more than I'd been given. Fate had decided what my life would be, not because of what I deserved or didn't deserve, but because fate could be cruel like that.

Now, I had made a choice to tell fate to fuck right off. Or accept what fate had been driving me to all along.

He walked closer, to the point where the light from

inside the house illuminated him. His eyes squinted, as if the light was too bright, or he couldn't decide if this was a new part in a game I was playing.

"You know I don't want just sex with you, right?" His voice was low, almost a whisper. "Don't get me wrong, I want to fuck you until we become a part of the stars, but that's not all I want. I want the whole thing, baby—the sex, the relationship, even the love."

I shivered at that last word. I wasn't sure what love was. Wasn't it just enhanced lust for a man? Or was it that need to see them that made me feel like my guts had twisted inside of my belly? Was it the way my heart felt soft when he made me laugh and the way I didn't want that laughter to end?

"I don't know what I can give you, Aleric. I'm not made for this stuff. You should know that by now. I don't trust this whole mating thing either." I stopped when I realized his face had fallen. I'd given him the wrong idea, damn! "I can try though."

"Really?" he asked softly, his eyes lighting up with dragon fire.

I felt my own blaze in response, a sensation of heat that was pleasant, not painful.

"I can't promise I'll be any good at it. I'll probably suck at relationships as much as I suck at being soft." I floundered around in my head for something more to say, something that didn't make me sound like a loser. "All I can do is try."

I held my hand out to him, a plea on my face and in my eyes. Understand. Help. Show me how to do this. I'd never been a mate, or a girlfriend. I didn't know anything about living with other people either. I'd been on my own since I left home all those years ago. The only relationship I had was with my boss and sometimes I talked to the woman who checks on my apartment when I'm away on missions.

I took a deep breath and did what he had apparently been waiting on. I stepped toward him, and he took my hand at last. He pulled me close, close enough to smell his scent, and I inhaled every particle of it that I could. Instead of a kiss, we melted into each other; my nose in his neck, his in my hair. Our arms twined around each other, and we stood in the darkness, clasped together as we let the mating bond take us over.

"I promise you I will make your life a joy. We might have arguments, there may be danger, but I will do all that I can to make your life a happy one. And to fight whatever fight it is you're a part of. I am yours, as you are mine. Together, we will make this work."

I stared up at him, and for the first time in my life, I didn't feel alone. At all.

5

leric didn't say a single word more as he walked into the light at last. I stepped back until I felt the couch against the backs of my legs. I didn't fall, I just stood there and looked at him. Something built inside of me, some emotion I wasn't familiar with. Aleric pushed me down gently to the couch and followed behind me.

He nestled himself between my thighs and looked down at me. My skin gleamed as he brushed a hand up my calf, then over my thigh, before he pushed up the edge of the shirt I wore, just enough to see me. I held my breath and waited to see what he'd do. *How good was this going to be,* I wondered? I had a feeling incredible was the only word that would suit.

He pulled at me and I moved, my hips tilted up, and my thighs spread wider.

His fingers slid up my left thigh, and up over my hip, to settle just below my belly button. I inhaled sharply, and my bottom lip shivered at the innocent but so erotic, unfamiliar touch. I realized then that Aleric hadn't touched me anywhere but on my breast the night before. That had been all it took for him to rock me.

What would he do next?

"Do you want me, Edana?" he asked quietly while his fingers stroked at the silky skin of my abdomen.

"You know I do, Aleric." I didn't have the patience for more words, I wanted him to touch me *there. Now!*

I didn't have to wait long. I gasped as a finger traced down my abdomen and into my most private flesh, flesh that nobody had touched recently. I knew in that moment no other person would ever touch me there again. Only him.

I began to smell his dragon scent as his skin heated with excitement. I was sure my pupils were huge at this point, and I could tell my nostrils had flared.

I was terrified of what I was about to do, curious about how it would change me, but most of all it aroused me to the point of desperation. And he'd only slid his finger between my folds. He hadn't done anything else.

I looked up to see his eyes were on my face, and I lost myself in their blue color. That was, until he twitched that finger and his palm pressed into the most sensitive part of me. Only a twitch, but it was enough for the very end to slide into me, only an inch, but we both felt it.

Neither of us spoke, we just watched the other, waited, and breathed. Without words or the frantic whispered moans for more, I could actually hear the way his breathing changed as his finger slid a little deeper, only a little. I could tell how much he was aroused by how wet my pussy was, how tight and hot I was. Only for him.

His fingers slid deeper into the depths of my wetness, and I inhaled sharply again. How much more of this could I stand?

His fingers were long and strong, and his touch was inquisitive. I was sure my eyes were round with fascination and awe at my own bravery, because now I'd given myself to him and was about to make it totally complete. I felt my dragon curl somewhere around my spine, then stretch out into my head to blaze out of my eyes. Aleric's flared in response. There was no going back now. I didn't even want to.

Aleric's other hand stroked my cheek before his fingers moved to my mouth.

He gently outlined my lips, caressed them, and I opened for him. I could breathe again, but now I breathed fast, harsh, as I tasted his finger on my tongue. His dragon flared in his eyes again. I smiled around his finger before I sucked it and heard him groan in delight.

The simple action had an effect, and that thrilled me. My legs squeezed together around his hand, and he pulled his finger from my mouth.

The wet finger moved over my chest, flicked at my nipples through my shirt, down my stomach, and I watched it track down. He pushed the shirt up and I moved, pulled it off, and threw it away. I wanted to be naked for him. His eyes went wide as he took me in.

My breasts were tipped with dark nipples, big enough to fill his hands, but not too large. A slim waist flared down to my hips. Hips that he gripped with that hand now.

"This is going to happen, Edana. You know that right? I'm going to slide into you." Aleric paused to slide his finger deeper, and I hitched in a breath that turned into a gasp. The finger was deep inside of me. It filled me but his sleepy eyes promised me he could fill me with something much better. "And I'm going to make you come in ways you didn't know were possible."

He pulled away, out of me, away from me, but only long enough to drop his clothes. Then he was back, and I felt his warm skin as his hands pushed my thighs apart. I thought he'd slide into me then, I was ready for that first miraculous touch of his length inside of me, but he surprised me again. Instead of giving me his cock, he moved down, pushed the coffee table back, and pulled my feet up to his shoulders.

"Oh my," I gasped and he grinned at me, a devilish grin that made my already liquefied insides twist into sharp need.

I felt his shoulders against my inner thighs, and then he kissed me just on my hip. Oh, I would have killed him if he didn't touch me somewhere more intimate soon. I wanted to squirm like an untried virgin, to beg for his touch, but all I could do was wrap my fingers in his blond hair and wait. I felt his breath as he moved down, at last, and the soft touch of his hot lips on my skin.

And then his tongue lapped at my folds, diving deep to split me open wide.

"Mmm." I heard a soft sound of appreciation. Apparently, he liked the way I tasted. Good, because the sensation of his tongue there had me near insanity.

My hands clutched at his hair as his tongue teased at my clit; the slick strokes were so *liquid,* so *good* that I wanted to grind my hips into his face until we both died from the pleasure of it all. My head fell back, and I knew I whispered his name, but it wasn't something I'd wanted to do. I just did it because I couldn't control myself now. That was all gone the second his tongue found me, wet and ready for his touch.

I pushed my ass deeper into the couch as his tongue worked its magic, and I knew it wasn't going to be long before I came apart. I needed to come. I was so close, if he'd just take it that little bit of an edge further.

I gasped and panted. I needed one more thing to push me over, just a little more pressure! "Please, Aleric, I need..."

His tongue pushed harder onto my clit and I felt the first pulse explode inside of me as it stole my breath away. My hips moved of their own will as they followed the source of my pleasure.

Aleric didn't seem to mind because he kept stroking the tiny bundle of nerves between my legs. He groaned against me, which only sent me even higher. I'd left even my dragon behind now, and I didn't care. All I felt was the pleasure of Aleric's tongue on me. I thought I'd die of suffocation! I couldn't breathe, I was so caught up in the bliss he'd given me. Everything had stopped—time, colors, the world. All there was in the world now was this exquisite release that my mate had given me.

I came back to the world and could hear a keening sound. It took a moment to realize it was me, but as the pleasure started to recede and my dragon pulled me back down, I breathed, and the sound stopped.

Without another word, Aleric grabbed my face to watch my eyes as he slid into me. His face was harsh with concentration as he ate up every sign of my reaction to him. When he knew he had my attention, his fist went into my hair to pull my head back so that he could look deeper. That's when he slid deeper. He stretched me he was so thick, and I began to wonder if he'd ever bottom out, but then he did and we both sighed in fulfillment.

Our dragons moved, and we were one at last. With a heavy groan he began to move. Slow and deep, then hard and fast as my breath quickened. I felt every inch of him as he pushed into me, every single inch, and the withdrawals were their own pleasure. Whether in or out, Aleric caressed my walls in just the right way.

He changed his pace each time my breath changed. He went deeper, harder, without a single plea from me. My hips moved, we found the right rhythm, and then we were two dragons, two souls, four entities combined into one as the world around us disappeared into the fire that we created together. Flames licked at me, at my nipples, at my lips, at my eyes as we came apart together. I knew those flames were Aleric, just as the flames that touched him were me. I felt his lips on mine, his tongue on mine, but knew it was the flames.

The sensation of being touched in every single part of my body by his flames drove me into a world that did not exist, into nothing, into something I'd never suspected existed. Pure bliss and nothing more.

The world came back slowly, much more slowly this time, and I wondered if there'd come a time when we didn't come back. Why did we want to go back when this world was perfect?

He sank down to my chest, still on his knees, and I

held him close to my body. We both shook from the experience. Neither of us could say a single word. Words didn't exist yet, but they would. Later, I'd explore him. I'd find out how to make him make that sound again, that one that spurred me into dirty thoughts. For now, I tried to catch my breath and not die from completion.

Eventually, he stirred and lifted me to take me into the bathroom. There, he ran a bath and washed me gently. From my head to my toes, Aleric washed every single part of me. We didn't talk, still; there were no words for what had just happened. There was only a glance to say thank you, a kiss to express appreciation, a touch to say we are one now.

Words weren't needed when you were one being. I knew his thoughts, and he knew mine. For now, I couldn't keep him out, but I had the secrets still locked away. Somehow. I breathed a sigh of relief and got out of the tub. I dried off while he washed himself.

I watched, in love with the sight of him, with him. How could I not adore a body made powerful by his lifestyle, by his dragon? Every inch of him was sculpted into perfection, and I loved every inch. From the thick calves and powerful thighs, to the strong arms and vigorous chest that were made for me to cuddle into: Aleric was perfect.

It wasn't just the sex though. I loved his soul, the one

that wasn't sure about his father, or why he still felt loyalty to the man. I loved the poetry within him, the softness of his emotions, the fierceness of his love. Aleric wasn't a total milksop after all; he was a poet in a soldier's body. His body, his mind, reflected that perfectly.

"You are beautiful, Edana," he said as he got out of the tub.

Words were back then. I smiled at him and handed him a towel.

"I guess that means we both are then. I was just admiring how perfect you are." I couldn't stop smiling. Even if I sounded like an idiot, I could not stop feeling happy.

"Hardly perfect, but I will try my best to be for you." His fingers traced down my jaw as he tilted my face up for his kiss.

I opened my mouth when his tongue probed at my lips, let him inside, but I wanted something else on my tongue. I dropped to my knees.

"You don't have to..." he began, but I stopped him with a crooked eyebrow and my hand on his cock.

"I know I don't have to, Aleric. I fucking want to. I've wanted to from the moment I met you. Let a girl fulfill a fantasy or two, won't you?"

It had been awhile since I'd had sex, and I'd never fucked a dragon before, but there was a first time for everything. I tasted him with my lips at first, and his knees nearly bucked. A deep grunt from him made my insides twist, but I ignored it. I wanted more of those.

I thought he'd bury his hands in my hair, but instead, his fingers moved to my lips, and he held his cock as I moved down its length. I took him deeper, sucked at him, until he made that sound again. When I moved back up his cock, his fingers followed. I sucked at the tip, and he nearly dropped to his knees, but he stayed up.

"Edana, please, baby, let me…"

But I didn't want that. I wanted his taste on my tongue and refused to budge.

I was shameless with my need for his pleasure but didn't care. I needed it, I needed to taste him. I was too hungry for it to stop. I grabbed his ass with both of my hands and held him to my face as I moved on him, greedily taking every inch he had to give me.

There were a million places inside of me that pulsed with each one of those groans of his, and I wanted more. I might die of shame if I came on my knees while I sucked him off, but it'd be some time later. Right now, I just needed all he had to give me.

I glanced up to see a smug smile on his face. I hadn't expected that.

"Hungry, darling?"

I squinted at him and sucked harder. The smugness

disappeared into a rapt look of amazement as I felt his cock pulse in my mouth. Oh, there we go!

Pleasure coursed through me as his hot liquid spilled onto my tongue. I tasted his dragon on his essence. I tasted him—the real Aleric—and it was better than my favorite ice cream. His hips twitched, and he gave this low sound that stretched out incredibly long. It made all of those achy places inside of me go haywire, and I felt my walls begin to pulse without even the slightest touch from either of us.

I drank down every drop of my mate, and then I sank to the floor. I didn't have anything else to give just then.

6

───────

The next morning, I woke up sore and tired but satisfied. Kind of. Aleric was pressed into me, his body heat a temptation I could not resist. I turned in his arms, and he kissed me as his arms grasped me tightly to his body.

I turned to him, sought out his heat, and I murmured a sigh of happiness as his tongue slid over mine. His left hand went over my waist to slide onto my ass.

His strong fingers kneaded the muscles there while he pushed me into the thigh he'd pressed between mine. I couldn't stop when my hips twisted against the warm flesh there and lost myself in the pleasure of Aleric kissing me.

I was still half asleep, but his touch aroused a primal part of my brain. That dragon part that said sleep was for the weak.

I ran my hands down his arm. I wanted to feel his cock in my hand, to make him groan again and press into me as I stroked him. I had so many naughty wants, but I knew I'd get to do them all, eventually.

No matter how many times I heard those intoxicating sounds Aleric made I could never get enough of them. "Turn around."

He gave me a confused look but did as I asked. When his back was to me, I slid my hand down his hip and felt a shiver go through his body. He knew what I wanted to do. I smiled because I knew he'd let me do it. I was patient when he wanted to do something to me, when he wanted to make me explode; it was my turn now.

I found him hard and ready for my touch. I gripped his cock tight, but not too tight.

"I thought you wanted to fuck, Edana?" he asked as his hand went over mine. He didn't move to stop me though, only to show me the pace he liked best.

"There's always next time, Aleric. I want this for now, to jerk you off, because it's been on my mind since I met you," I whispered into his ear, nipping at the side of his neck to tell him to be quiet and stop protesting.

I ran my tongue along the edge of his ear and heard him sigh. His hips began to move with the rhythm of my hand. His breath came faster, and I knew he was close. *How much would it take,* I wondered, as I stroked the hot silk in my fist. How hard would he come when he came?

I pressed my hips into him, my own deep ache almost a pain. A good kind of pain, though. Later, I knew he'd tease me to within an inch of my life, but for now, I had him in my thrall.

"You know it's only you who can do this to me, right, Edana? There's no other person alive who will ever be able to make me feel like you do." His words came out on a harsh whisper that trembled near the end. He was close.

"Nobody, Aleric? Ever?" I asked, my fingers tight on his cock as I spoke with a harsh whisper. I hadn't realized until he said the words just how much I needed to hear them.

"Only you, Edana. Only you, baby!" Aleric gasped as his hips moved faster, and I knew he was on the edge.

"Then come for me, baby. Show me what you are only ever going to give to me and me alone." I felt so much power in that moment, so much control, with his dick in my hand, his body wrapped in mine. It was an amazing sensation, and something I'd never done before.

It was intimate, one of those things you would only share with someone who was your partner, but Aleric was more than my partner; he was my mate.

His gasp told me he was close, and I wasn't surprised when his head fell back against my shoulder. I kissed my way down his jawline, prickly now without a shave.

I whispered to him about just how much I adored him and the things I wanted to do with him. Aleric gave a soft sound somewhere between a sigh and a groan as he pulsed in my hand. He shivered in my arms as my hand moved over him.

My breath caught in my throat when he turned over after his shivers stopped, and I caught the full brunt of his beautiful eyes. Love blazed in those eyes and desire that would never die, no matter how many times we quenched our need. I gazed into those blue depths until his head moved forward to catch my lips.

A long, low moan escaped my lips, and he breathed the sound in, his lips hot on mine.

His hands went to my breasts, and I pressed them deeper into his hands. Aleric loved them, and he'd slept with one hand cupped over them for most of the night.

Then he slid down my body, and I forgot what I was supposed to be thinking about.

Aleric's lips were wonderfully full and sucked expertly at my pussy, explored it from top to bottom with guttural sighs of enjoyment.

I moved against his face, my pussy swollen with pleasure as he finally got his fingers into me. They slid deep inside of me without hesitation and my back arched against the softness of the bed.

"Fuck, Aleric. Baby, that feels so good," I gasped but cried out a nonsound when his fingers found my nipples. He tugged at them tightly, just the way he knew I liked. A point that was almost painful, but not quite.

Aleric didn't reply, he just went after my clit, and his tongue flicked at it in a steady tempo that made my hips bounce. I was going to die, fuck, I was going to die from how good it felt!

I hadn't come yet, but I could feel it coming, that breathless feeling that somehow turned into too much air and then none at all as the pleasure broke over me. Aleric sent me over an edge that would kill me one day, I just knew it woud, but that didn't stop me seeking it out with every part of me.

"Aleric!" I cried and wrapped my legs around his head with total abandon.

When the fiery world of our dragons was gone, when I'd come back to the real world, he moved, our lips met, and he kissed me hard and deep. He pressed me into the bed with fierce, sudden need.

Aleric kissed me deeply, his tongue tangled with mine seductively, and I knew we weren't done, not yet.

I didn't know what I should say or do? Something romantic and sweet? That's not who I was. Something seductive? I could pull that off, or even sensual, but sweet and romantic? Best to just kiss him and not worry about words that might ruin it all because I was just too damned goofy to be sweet.

"What's wrong?" he whispered against my jaw, and I

rolled my eyes behind closed eyelids. He caught my thought then.

Sort of. Maybe I'd tensed or something. "Nothing, Aleric, this just isn't what I'm used to."

"What isn't?" I could hear the confusion in his voice. "This wasn't the first time you've been with a man, what's different?"

"You're still here. I've usually run them off by the time the sun comes up. I've never..." I paused as a moment of embarrassment took my breath away. Not because I was ashamed of my past but because I wasn't used to admitting things like this. "I've never *wanted* anyone to stay through the night."

"Until me?"

"Until you, Aleric. You're the only man I've ever woken up with." The fact that he was more than a simple man went unsaid. It was a given.

"Then I hope it's something you want to get used to." His voice held the amusement his grin showed. I stroked a finger down his jawline, inhaled the scent of our exertions, and wanted more.

"I don't want anything else. I'll have to go back to work at some point," I hurried to add that last bit when his face fell. "For now though, I'm yours, Aleric."

I didn't want anything else right now, and that's what I'd been afraid of since I'd met him. That I'd lose my sense of responsibility to my job, that I'd lose myself in him.

"You're such an independent woman, Edana. It must be hard to give that up, to become one out of two."

"I had a mother and father for a while, and then a grandmother, but even she passed away." I paused, and he broke into my train of thought.

"What happened to your father? I assume he must have been the dragon since your mother was part of the slayer clan."

"He was. I don't know what happened to him. He wasn't much of a father." I turned to my side, to block him —all of it—out, to curl into myself and ignore the hurt of the past. "He just disappeared one day and I was alone. I stayed that way until somebody figured out he was gone and I was at the house by myself. It wasn't long, a few days."

"Long enough to know loneliness and misery, I have to assume," he responded, his hand on my shoulder.

"Long enough, yes."

"When you're ready, you can tell me who you work for. What it is you do, exactly. I won't pressure you about it. I'm part of my father's defense, but I've also spent a lot of time studying our worlds. I know there are organizations out there..."

"So there are. But that's not what we're here for is it?" I turned back, a smile in place. I wanted to hide so much from him, and his words told me he was too close to a correct guess about what I did.

It was my job to hide what I did from the world, to keep it safe, to try to keep so many worlds safe.

I'd decided to take this leap with Aleric, mainly because my body refused to comply with my brain, and I'd been unable to resist him any longer.

"I never knew gray could be such a beautiful color, until I met you, Edana," he whispered as he slid my body beneath his and looked into my eyes. "It's such a murky color, so obviously colorless, but in your eyes, it's the most beautiful color in the world."

His lips slid down my jaw again, and once more the world disappeared and there was only us. He slid into me with one stroke, without a single moment of preamble, and I didn't need it. I only needed him.

My nails clawed at his back, my body moved in time with his, and in moments we were flames and nothing more. The world around us burned, our dragons twisted together, and I wondered if he'd take every part of me, even my fear of heights, so that I could shift at last.

I'd never been able to before, even though I could feel my dragon-self there, beside my slayer-self. Within me, I should have been a mess, a mass of confusion as my two halves tried to battle each other, but somehow it hadn't happened. My selves had been compliant with each other since I'd been conceived. I just wasn't very good at being a dragon.

I could read minds, when I really tried. I could control fire with my hands, which were both slayer weapons, but I was also very strong and healthier than humans or slayers. My skin was tougher, my bones stronger, and I'd never suffered infections. My body was dragon strong, even if I couldn't become one.

And now, it was a part of Aleric, two dragons turned into one within the world we'd set on fire. I twisted in the flames, lost to the pleasure of his dragon's touch. The flames did not burn me, could not burn me, for I was a dragon too. They could only touch me with heat and sensuality.

Being with Aleric wasn't just about losing myself in pleasure, though, it was about that moment when I wrapped myself in him and let more into my mind than my own thoughts. When the world came back I found it hard to let go of Aleric. I wanted to stay there, as if intoxication had become addiction. I should be afraid of that yearning, I knew I should, but I couldn't be. Aleric makes it so simple to sink away from it all. I could stay there in that perfect world. If only I'd allow us to.

"I have to get back to my own world at some point too," he said after a long moment of silence.

"I hadn't thought about that. You're a prince, I assumed that's all you did really. I know you're a soldier, but as a prince you're not allowed to go into harmful situations, are you?" I rolled away from him and propped my head up on my hand to watch him.

"Oh, on the contrary. I'm expected to be on the front lines with my siblings and the rest of the fighters. There's no shirking of duty and publicity shots for us. We're the real deal. If we want to stay in power, we have to fight for it."

*That was far easier to get out of him than it should have been,* my internal interrogator said. Mate or not, Aleric should guard such information from even me. He didn't want to, it seemed, and verbally volunteered the information. Which made me wonder just how much of this little tale I'd divulge to my boss. Then he kissed my neck and began to tickle me, and I let the whole mess disappear as we laughed our way into getting out of bed.

7

The dynamics of our relationship had changed when we became lovers. I knew I wouldn't ever want to fuck another man for the rest of my life, and that I'd given him the ability to make me want something more from my life. He'd told me he had to go back to his own life soon, but we hadn't talked about what we would do with ourselves after we left this place. I'd made it obvious I didn't plan to leave my life, and he had his own life to live.

That complicated our relationship, but we'd gone from two people who had been made mates by fate, to two people whom I was certain had started to fall in love with each other. I watched him later that evening, our second evening on the island, and wondered where we'd be in a week, or a month even.

He was busy building a fire in a ring of stones on

the sand. We'd been out there, under a canopy of palm trees, for most of the day. I'd spread a couple of blankets on the grass, dropped the pretext of being modest, and sprawled out naked to absorb the warmth into my body. After so much time spent wrapped up in layers and huddled next to a stove, the ability to absorb warmth from the air was a wonderful thing.

The fire was to keep bugs away and to set a romantic mood. Aleric had a nice flame by the time he came and snuggled up behind me.

Obviously, my mate had decided he wanted to fuck me again, because I felt his cock pressed into my ass, hard and ready.

"Oh, Aleric, are you never satisfied?" I teased.

"We have to go back to the real world soon. I don't know how long it will be before I can see you again." I noted a tone of concern there, and that worried me. Would he be in trouble for being gone so long? "Let me love you, Edana. Help me to forget that world," he whispered, his lips on that spot on the back of my neck that made me weak for him. Why was he so worried about going home? I had to wonder, but his teeth nipped at that spot and I didn't even know there was another world anymore.

I felt heat begin to flow through me as he continued to tease my neck. My head fell forward to give him better access, and he pushed a hand between my thighs to seek out the wet heat there.

"Let me make you come, Edana. It makes the world a perfect place when you moan my name," Aleric said, his knee a wedge between mine.

I shifted one leg over his while he positioned my hips to make it possible to slide up into me. It was an awkward position, I was still on my side and Aleric was inside of me but still behind me. Despite how awkward it was, how very exposed I felt, it let me feel every centimeter of him as he slid into me. And even the fact that any passing plane or boat could see us wasn't a deterrent. In fact, it made the whole situation that little bit naughty and made my brain pulse even more.

I moved with my mate, my movements snakelike as they followed the rhythm he set. I lost my mind as Aleric nipped at that spot on the back of my neck again, his left hand between my thighs to tease me even higher. I couldn't think at all; all I could do was feel every spot where he touched me.

I moved with him, so lost I didn't even make noises, just moved in time with him as I felt him move behind me, within me, as we went deeper and deeper into the world of pleasure.

His arms wrapped around me, and his fingers went to my nipples as the darkness around us turned to bright colors of pleasure.

"Don't stop, Aleric. Baby, please, that's it," I managed to gasp out before my world exploded.

I felt his hand as it slid down between my folds; his fingers were hot against my clit.

"You're so amazing, Edana," he whispered against my ear.

"Mmmm." It was the only response I could give before I felt my walls pulse around his length, a pulse that seemed to follow the pull of his lips while they sucked at my neck.

I pushed his hand away as the pleasure became too much and pulled away from his lips at my neck.

I pushed until he fell back, and I straddled his hips to ride him. His head fell back into the sand, and his eyes closed with a sigh as I slid my slick heat down to surround him.

I sighed with relief as he filled me and clenched my muscles to give him an extra squeeze.

I smiled as his gasps turned to groans. I twitched my hips just right, just the way he liked, and slid up a bit just to come right back down on him. I began to grind on him, a slick, delicious pace that had us both breathless and eager for what was to come. At the same time, neither of us seemed to be in a hurry to up the pace. We had all the time in the world, in that moment, at least.

His hands clasped at my hips and I looked down into dragon eyes. Eyes that burned with a love unlike anything I'd ever known before. That desire-filled look took my breath away, made my heart clench, and I was lost. My hips slowed, and my right hand clenched somewhere over his heart, as if to steal it from his very chest.

It wasn't until then that I knew I'd always wanted love like that, that I'd needed it. It was only Aleric who could give it to me, though. Only him who could love every part of me. He didn't have to say the words, they were there in the way his eyes adored me. I could picture us, this Greek-godlike creature, and me, the dark-haired woman with wide hips, my hair brushing at his thighs, as we worked together for perfection.

I loved him then, totally, completely, without reservation and I felt something change within me, something broke and I wanted to scream with relief. Instead, I moaned as the world became pure rapture.

Aleric had broken me, he had healed me, and later I'd figure out just what it all meant. For now, I could only ride the waves he followed me on. I couldn't breathe, I could only feel, and when his hands tightened on my hips, when he growled my name, the world turned into flames once again.

"Are you hungry?" he asked as the flames burned out in the stone circle. Where he'd found stones on an island I didn't know, but it didn't seem important. Maybe it was a volcanic island and they'd spewed up from the depths of the earth, liquid that was thousands of years old now cooled to stones.

"I could eat," I murmured, on my stomach as I stared into the dying flames. I wasn't really interested in eating, I was too caught up in watching the flames as they danced in the circle.

"What would you like?" His hand on my bottom caught my attention as awareness filled me once more.

"Pizza?" I knew we didn't have it, but it was the first thing that came to mind.

"Hmmm. No, not today. What else?"

"Potato salad and smoked sausage?"

"I see a theme here. High carbs, and a short wait time. I think I get the picture." I heard the smile in his voice and smiled back.

"Omelet it is then?" I'd learned he was great at omelets when we were in the cabin.

"Probably. Let's go look." He pulled me up with him, and we went into the house. I paused as we made it to the kitchen and sat down.

There was a fuzzy feeling in the back of my mind, a sensation that I knew meant Arista was trying to reach me. I almost allowed the invasion of my mind, but when I saw the way Aleric smiled as he looked into the fridge,

I knew I couldn't let our time go. Not yet. I blocked the invasion abruptly and turned back to him.

It was something I'd have never thought about doing before, not so abruptly, but now, I wanted the privacy we had. I knew what his father had done to his brothers when they found their mates, knew how he'd almost killed Arista and Malcolm, and I wanted this moment of peace. His father would no doubt make trouble for us too. I wanted this time without the world to invade our tranquility.

"That would be amazing!" I said when he pulled a bowl of pasta salad out of the fridge.

"What else?" he asked as he put the bowl down and went back to inspect the contents.

"Just this. It's high in carbs, but I think we'll burn them right back off again, don't you?" I pulled the plastic from the glass bowl and found two forks in the drawer by the sink before I went back to the stool at the island.

The kitchen was a sea of white, from cabinets to the appliances; even the floor was white marble. It was a bit bright during the day, but at night it gleamed in a way I liked. This island might be my favorite place ever. I loved every room and the seclusion of it. It was like I'd decorated the place myself, and it was perfect.

"You're sure?" He poured white wine into a glass and then one of red for him.

"Yep." I popped a forkful of the food into my mouth

and began to chew. I hadn't realized I was so hungry, but now we ate quietly until the bowl was empty. I speared a tiny sliver of pickle with my fork and popped it into my mouth. "This is perfect. I thought I was the only person who put pickles in this stuff."

"I guess not." Aleric had a smile on his face that said he had a secret.

I went still and glared at him. "What are you not telling me?"

"I had it all made for you," he began but then stopped. He inhaled deeply, thought about his next words, and then carried on. "I can't read most of your thoughts, but when it comes to food, you're quite open with what you prefer. I let the cook know how you liked it."

"Oh." I could only stare at him. He'd admitted something I thought we'd never talk about, that I blocked him from my thoughts. On purpose.

I felt guilty about it. He was so very open with his own, but even then, I knew there were a few walls that blocked something from me. His entire mind wasn't a steel trap though, not like mine was.

"One day, Aleric. One day I'll be able to let the walls down. Maybe." I put my hand over his on the island, and we didn't say anything else about it. What could we say? We both knew those secrets were worth protecting.

"It's alright, Edana. I just wish..." he paused and stood

up. "Well, there's no use wishing is there? Want to watch a movie?"

"Zombie Island of Death?" I joked with a laugh.

"Is that a real movie?" he asked seriously, and I laughed.

"No, darling. Not at all. What do you want to watch?" He hated horror movies, but I loved them. I couldn't help it. Sometimes it was nice to know people could escape nightmares, that was all.

"There's one about a deer, a cartoon, I think. I've heard about it, but I've never seen it."

I stared at him. "*Bambi?*" I was certain my face was a mask of astonishment, I couldn't help it. "Are you talking about *Bambi?*"

"That sounds right. Yes. Can we watch that one?"

I could only stare at him. Here was this big tough man with battle scars, one in particular on his arm that must have been deep when it happened. And he wanted to watch a Disney movie?

"Sure." Maybe his escape from a nightmare world was fantasy. "I'm not sure you'll like it all. There are parts..."

"Don't tell me. I want to find out for myself." He made his way into the bedroom, fiddled with the flat-screen television, and joined me on the bed.

I curled around his chest, my leg over his hips, as the movie played on. I'd only ever done this with Aleric.

Another first. I felt safe, something else I hadn't realized before. I'd always been on edge, always on alert. Here, we couldn't be found, nobody could intrude, and I was totally relaxed for the first time in what may have been my entire life.

I fell asleep on his chest, the sound of his dragon heart strong beneath my ear. When my dreams came, they were of a future that was just like this. Peaceful and tranquil.

The dream turned dark, however, when storm clouds rolled in and a drum beat began to fill the air. Something about the beat seemed sinister, evil, and I wanted to run. Aleric held me by my hand, and we stood together to face the black fog that soon accompanied the clouds. A thick, hot fog. Smoke, not fog at all. I woke up with a cough that hacked at my lungs.

There was something coming, something bad, but as Aleric curled around me in the dark, I knew we'd face it together. We might not overcome it, but we'd face it together. I closed my eyes and the images came again. The world wasn't safe; it was in terrible danger. This time of peace wouldn't last. Would we survive what was headed our way? I trembled and put Aleric's hand under my cheek. Together, I reminded myself. Together we could face anything.

8

—————

"Fuck…" I cried out the word on a loud sigh of relief as Aleric's tongue sucked out the last wave of pleasure my body could possibly produce. "Fuck… fuck, fuck, fuck."

*He'd proven me wrong in so many ways,* came a stray thought as I stared up at the reed ceiling. I thought bones were solid but mine were sludge. I thought you could never come too much, I thought, eventually, my orgasms would ebb down to a 'that's nice' level, but he'd just blown my mind again. I thought you could never be fucked stupid… well, there I was, my eyes glazed and my brain all but empty. *Breathe,* I reminded myself, *slow and easy, breathe.*

I flopped a hand in his general direction when he moved up beside of me with a grin. I let my head loll to his side of the bed, my face expressionless. I couldn't find the energy to make one, not even a smile.

"I might be dead," I drawled between dry lips. My eyes closed. If this was death, I wasn't so afraid of it after all.

"You aren't." I heard him chuckle, and reality began to intrude again. I almost felt real sensation in my fingertips. I didn't want that. I wanted to linger in the calm place of no pain, no fear, no worry.

"I could be. If you tried harder."

"I don't think you really want me to fuck you to death, do you?" he asked with another soft chuckle, his hand splayed on my abdomen.

"Maybe. If that's what it feels like." I finally mustered up enough energy to grin at him.

"Mmm, it is nice, isn't it?"

"So good," I corrected, and moved to kiss him. He tasted of mint and orange juice. "I guess that means I have to get up?"

"No, you can stay here. But I wanted to explore the other side of the island today."

"Oh. I'll come too." I sat up, scooted over the expanse of the huge bed, and headed for the bathroom. "Let me get cleaned up and dressed."

"No rush," he called.

I ducked under the shower to wash off and brush my teeth, dried off, twisted my hair into a bun, threw on some shorts and a tank top, and ran into the living room with a pair of trainers that I shoved my feet into.

"Ready."

I saw he had two rucksacks packed, and he took the heavier black bag. I picked up the red one and followed him out.

"The island isn't very big, so it shouldn't take long," I said, just to break the silence.

We didn't always talk a lot, we didn't always have to; a look or a gesture was enough to communicate most of the time. I liked that, but today, the silence irked me a little.

"No, but I brought a tent, in case you want to stay on that side." He led the way, and I couldn't keep my eyes off the round, tight muscles of his ass and legs.

Who knew men could have gorgeous legs? I did now. Aleric wore long, khaki colored shorts that hugged his bottom and showed off just how muscular his legs were. Nice, thick calves, not the sticks some poor fellas had. These were the legs of an active man, one who worked hard and played rough.

"Do you have sports in your world?" I asked, wondering what kind of games he might be interested in.

"You mean like your rugby and basketball?" he called over his shoulder. "We've got one similar to rugby, but not the rest. Some of the younger generations might start a version of basketball; it's become popular to go to your world to watch it."

"Oh." My organization didn't know about these excursions. That troubled me. Why hadn't we known the young dragons were coming to our world? And did that mean there was more we didn't know about?

"I like the rugby. I play sometimes, with the men and women in my unit." He paused, but then went on. I couldn't see his face, so I didn't know what the pause meant. Maybe I just needed a breath since we were climbing a steep hill. "It's fun. I like the competitiveness, but I hate the aches the next day. We aren't as careful as you are in your world, even with a game as rough as rugby."

"Oh," I said again. Rugby was a fairly rough sport. I'd seen men playing in bloody bandages with fairly large bruises before. My romantic poet liked rough sports? I liked that idea.

"We're nearly to the top now. We'll be able to see the whole island from up here. We can go down to the other side after." Aleric continued to lead the way, and I followed along behind.

I cried out when my foot slid on some soft sand and started to fall. Normally, I was more coordinated, but just as I'd set my foot down, Arista blasted me with a psychic wave so powerful I was knocked off balance. *Where are you, and where is Aleric?* screeched through my head like a tidal wave of Arista's voice. I would have fallen to the ground but Aleric caught me.

"She get you too?" he asked with a rueful smile.

"Just a little," I admitted. "She's getting a bit insistent."

"I'll take care of it. Come on, come look at this view." He helped me to brush sand off my palms and knees before we carried on.

At the very top of the hill was a plateau, flat and round. From here, there was nothing but ocean, as if the entire world was an ocean. Maybe it was? Aleric could have brought me to a world where the Earth was still forming, where this was the only ground. *The air would be different though, wouldn't it?* I wondered as I looked around. I looked up to the sky and saw none of the tell-tale signs of planes there, and couldn't see any signs of boats, oil rigs, or other structures. We really could be in a different world.

"I don't want to leave this place, you know?"

"Better than the ice world, is it?" Aleric chuckled and went to a stone to sit down. I joined him, flat on the ground, and looked around.

We weren't too far up, but we were high enough that a breeze lifted stray strands of dark hair from around my face and blew them around my head. The breeze cooled my heated skin, and I fell back onto my pack. "I could stay here forever."

A scent floated in on the breeze, some tropical citrus

scent that made my stomach growl with yearning. Was it a flower, or was it Aleric? I could smell him, mixed in with that scent. I held my hand out to him and when he took it, I smiled up at him. "Maybe we should forget the world out there. You don't want to be king, do you?"

"No, and I'll have to take my father's place if Malcolm and Henry are out of the picture."

"What about Mary? Isn't she older than you?" I glanced down at our fingers twined together with a smile. This was what I'd dreaded? This feeling of being complete, at last?

"She took herself out of line a long time ago. And she's only a few months older than me; she's thirty and I'm twenty-nine. She doesn't want the crown and because Father had three sons, it was allowed."

"I see. So you're going to be the next king then?" I wasn't sure I liked that. It was something I'd forgotten until that blast from Arista. Of course they'd all be looking for him now and would be panicked if they couldn't find him.

"If something doesn't change soon, I suppose I will be the next in line." He didn't sound any happier about it than I felt.

"Don't you want to be king?" I prompted before I sat up to spread a blanket or two out for us to sit on. The ground was soft sand, but it would get everywhere.

He joined me on the red fleece blanket before he

answered. "There's something going on with my father. It's more than just the vampire blood, it has to be. He's just so... different now."

I paused, an eyebrow raised in question.

"He's not been himself for a while now. There are things..." Aleric paused again, his eyes closed and a hand tucked under his head as a pillow. Flat on his back, he was a beautiful sight, but this was important, I could sense it. "There are things going on that I don't understand, and when I go back, I will get to the bottom of it all."

"I see." What else could I say? Aleric was volunteering information that could help me with my own work. Guilt twinged at my heart, but this could be vital information. I clenched his hand in mine, my eyes devouring every aspect of his features, and I waited. "What do you think is the root of the problem?"

"I have no idea. Maybe it's a form of dragon senility, brought on by the vampire blood. Father's well over three hundred years old now. Maybe it's old age." His fingers tensed on mine and he tugged at my hand. "Let's not talk about any of that anymore, Edana."

I rolled to his side, let my hair down, and gave him a smile. "Aren't you about done with all of that yet?"

He laughed and his hand came down on my hip to hold me tighter to his body. "If I live a thousand lifetimes, Edana, I'll never have enough of *that*. There's no such thing as enough of you, I'm certain of it. You are the light that makes the stars shine and the fire that makes the sunburn. You are the very air I breathe, Edana."

The laughter fled from us both as he spoke, and I could only stare. I didn't have a poet's soul or his words. I had words like, I like looking at you. You have a gorgeous face. My heart flips when I hear your voice first thing in the morning. I didn't have the fluency with emotion that my Aleric had and I was embarrassed to admit it.

I stroked his face with my index finger instead. I let my eyes tell him what my lips could not.

"I know, Edana. You're still here and I'm not dead. I know you feel the same way." His words were a reassurance that I hadn't failed him. "We've had very different lives. You had different lives from your family too, even if you won't tell me about that other part of your life. The job that's so important."

I kissed him to make the words stop, and we both knew it. I would not, could not, discuss my work with anybody outside of that sphere. He'd been a subject of our studies, in fact.

I stopped thinking about it the moment his lips met mine and felt a thrill at the plush softness of his lips. My fingers traveled down to the hem of his shirt and then beneath. I moaned in pure admiration as my fingers slid up the ridges of his abdominal muscles, then over his ribs, to flatten out over his heart. I felt it beating there, strong and steady, a promise that he would not leave me. As so many had before him.

For the first time in my life, I didn't want him to leave, I didn't want to be alone. "You are mine?"

"Always, Edana. Always yours and only yours." His lips brushed mine softly, but his fingers wiped away the tear that escaped from my eye. I hadn't even known it was there.

"We have to go home, to our own worlds…" I let the words trail off.

"I'm strong. I'll travel every night without a single complaint. For now, kiss me, my love." It didn't sound corny when he said it, it sounded sultry, provocative.

"No. I want to see the rest of the island. Come on, lazy bones. Let's get hiking." I stood up with a laugh and he rolled over on the blanket with a groan.

"You'll kill me one day." He grabbed my hand when I tried to roll him off of the blanket and pulled me back down to him. "We have time, Edana."

Time wasn't always guaranteed, I thought, but I let it slide. I accepted his kiss, and the embrace, and let him lead me through the steps that took me to that irresistible world that existed only for us. Passion was not a problem for us, only time was our enemy.

We found that place easily, quickly, and when it had

left us, we gathered our clothes from the area around the blanket with secret smiles. We'd made ourselves a public display, but it didn't matter. Only we existed here.

The other side of the island was more like a thick jungle, and there was no development at all. Our side had obviously been cleared to use as a base for the house and to utilize the beach.

"Arista keeps pinging me," he said as we pitched a tent for the night. We'd decided to stay on this side and watch the moon as it drifted across the sky. It was something I'd only ever done on my own, but it was hard to do in the city. Here, the sky was not only dark and free of light pollution, but the moon looked huge from wherever you were so you could see it on any part of the island freely.

"Can we do anything about it?" I sighed as we settled down around the campfire Aleric had lit in a pit of sand.

"We can talk to her, I suppose." He pulled a bottle of water from his bag and handed it to me. I took a sip before I answered him.

"Why are we hiding still?" I gulped another slug of water before I passed it back. "I know I've avoided them because I don't want to be interrupted. I don't want the real world to intrude on our time here."

"You didn't?" he asked, his voice quiet in an unusual way. As if he didn't want to hope.

"I haven't stayed put because you kidnapped me,

silly. I could have called for help at any time, you know. I stayed because I knew it was pointless to keep fighting what we had between us." I slipped beside him and brought his face down to mine so he could see me in the firelight. "I stayed because I wanted you, Aleric."

9

---

Stomach cramps are the worst. It was nature's way to tell me reality was out there. I'd convinced myself that we were the last people in the world, that we were alone and nothing could change that. Aleric had let Arista know we were fine, just taking some time to ourselves, and she'd left us to do just that. Now? Well, now nature reminded me of just how long I'd been gone and that I had to go back to it.

"You alright?" Aleric asked from his position beside me. We were sprawled on a blanket in the sand, absorbing the sun's heated rays and reading.

"Yeah, just girl problems," I said, and got up to take care of myself.

When I came back out, I'd changed into a light blue skirt I'd found in the closet, and it swirled around me as

I sat down. I stared out at the ocean from behind dark sunglasses.

"It's easy to think we're alone now, isn't it?" I sighed as he took my hand. "Can't we just stay here forever, and pretend those other worlds don't exist?"

"We could, but would we feel right doing that?" he prompted, and I turned to look at him.

"Responsibilities are heavy, aren't they?" I was thirty-five years old, but since we'd come to this island oasis, I'd forgotten. I felt like a teenager, without a care in the world. Every now and then I'd have a pang of guilt about what I *could* be doing, but not very often.

"It'll be alright, you'll see. When we go back, we'll go to see the places you've always wanted to see. I'll go with you to Italy, Germany, even to Thailand where there are other dragon myths."

"You remember that conversation?" We'd shared three bottles of wine that night, and I'd blathered on about the places I'd always wanted to travel to but hadn't got to yet. Mainly because my travels usually kept me in the United States.

"I remember every single one of our conversations, Edana." He sat up to look out at the ocean with me. "Maybe I should have a boat brought in, and we can sail around the island."

"That sounds nice." I stroked his fingers. "We have to go back soon though, Aleric. I can't avoid work forever."

"I know. I'll take you back, if you like?" His sadness was evident in his voice, in the way his hand went slack around mine.

"It can wait a few more days." I didn't even want to think about what might have happened while we were gone. I'd been working on gathering information for my boss. It just so happened that the target of that information was my own family.

I didn't feel bad about it, on the contrary, I felt as if my work helped to keep them safe. Something was going on with King Godwin, we all knew it, and I had a feeling it had something to do with the happenings in my own world. Vampires and shifters had started a war that very few knew about in the human realm.

Not long ago, an entire clan of wolves had been wiped out and the elders of my world had voted to put a stop to it. Because, yes, we had elders. None of my family knew about those little secrets, but I knew.

"Come on, let's go find something to eat," I said, and raced off to the house. I needed to distract myself, my thoughts, and cooking always did that for me.

I started a tomato sauce and the ingredients for fresh pasta. The pasta would take ages and would keep my mind occupied for a while. I washed my hands then went to the clean surface of the kitchen island and started to prepare the pasta.

"I remember this, I used to watch the cooks in the

kitchen when I was younger. You're making pasta?" He glanced at the pantry. "But there's some in there already."

"Oh, that's that dried-out garbage you should never eat. You'll love this and never eat dried pasta again. I promise." Then I thought about what he'd said. "Wait, you've had freshly made pasta and still like that garbage?"

I blinked at him, my fingers covered in the goo that would soon become flat sheets that I'd turn into strips of pasta.

He gave me a sheepish smile. "I can't tell a difference, really."

"I'm... well. I think I'm insulted." I went back to mixing ingredients. I glanced at him, then back. "Maybe don't say things like that when you've tasted mine? It'll be the best you've ever had, okay?"

He laughed, as I'd wanted him to, and asked if he could help with anything.

"No, go read or something. I'm going to be busy for a while." I shooed him out and went back to the pasta.

At least we had fresh ingredients and all of the food we could ever want here. I sighed, thinking about the problems of the world. If only people wouldn't try to control the magicals in our world, we could have so much. Instead, they'd been forced to hide away and became legends to scare children and grownups with.

My mate should be out helping to end world hunger. Instead, he had to fight to protect his existence from a world that would use him as a weapon. That was part of my job, to keep him and the humans from each other.

From what I'd learned, the Alexander brothers had taken care of most of the threat in our own world, all on their own, but there were other threats. Threats that meant human women had begun to disappear, never to be heard from again. Even their bodies hadn't been found.

I frowned and decided it was time to stop thinking about that stuff and focus on the pasta. When it formed a ball and had the right texture, I wrapped it in plastic and put it in the fridge to rest. While that was going, I started the sauce.

Vegetables became diced and sliced colors that were soon simmering in a pot. When the sauce was ready to go on low, my brain decided to pick up pieces of random thoughts I'd had over the last few weeks. Nature's little monthly present had reminded me that life will go on, must go on, and that mated or not, I had a life to get back to.

I took a bottle of wine from the fridge, poured a glass of white, and sat at a stool in front of my sauce. I glanced behind me to see that the living room was empty. Aleric must have gone outside or to the bedroom. Everything was done that could be, so I went into the living room and stared out at the ocean. Was this the calm before the storm? This sense of doom had started with the first cramp that twisted my insides this morning.

The sky was clear, the breeze gentle and cool, but I felt a darkness out there. Some menace that had yet to show itself to me. Was it just my own emotions and the fact we had to leave this place or was there more to worry about? Godwin had concerned me for some time now, but I didn't think the threat was from him. It felt bigger, meaner than a single entity that dared to impinge on my world.

It could, of course, just be me. I'd spent so long away from all that I knew, from all that seemed normal, that my mind interpreted it as a threat. I wasn't used to sleeping with anyone, literally sleeping not just sex. I wasn't used to talking about what I thought or how I felt with anyone, ever. Even my boss didn't know most of my thoughts, only what I reported to him about the matter at hand.

I could only sigh and wait for an answer to come.

"Edana, I think..." Aleric broke into my thoughts as he came into the living room. He paused, a look of pain twisted his features. "I think something's wrong. Arista and Malcolm are both on my case and won't let up."

"Then let them in." I was a bit confused about why

they'd pound away at him and not me. Perhaps they'd given up on contacting me.

I watched for a moment as Aleric's eyes went wide, then looked over at me. I could see him thinking a response back to whoever had him 'on the line', so to speak, and then he breathed deeply. Yeah, something was up.

"We need to go back tonight," he finally said, and sat down beside me. "It seems someone's been looking for you."

"Ah, probably my boss. Well, fuck. I wanted a few more days with you." I curled into his side and put my hand in his.

"I don't want to go back either. There's so much shit going on..."

I didn't push him to finish that thought. I knew there were secrets neither of us could talk about right now, but maybe one day we'd be able to share more about those. Even if it was my job to get the secrets out of Aleric.

I couldn't do that. He was my mate.

"When do we leave?" I sat up, my thoughts on the pasta. I could only assume it was my boss looking for me, and I wasn't in a rush to see him. I had even more secrets now, ones I couldn't share but should.

I'd write the normal report, but this time I'd keep it in my own filing cabinet, not the one at work.

"When the sun goes down, I guess. We need to eat then pack up."

"Alright, I'll get the pasta ready."

Reality was a bummer, maybe even more of a bummer than nature, I thought as I plated hot pasta later that evening. I poured the sauce over the dinner and we sat down for our last meal together in paradise. I looked out at the ocean, back at Aleric, and knew I'd changed. My entire world had changed, actually.

"You're bad for badassness, you know?" I teased with a smile. He looked up from his plate with a 'huh' expression. "I've turned into a woman with feelings and those are so gross, you know?"

"Trust the poet to fall for the woman with a heart of stone. A well-deserved one from what you've said, but still."

"It's not really falling though, is it?" I took a shaky breath before I continued. "We're mates, can there really be love when you're mates?"

"Of course there can. Mates hate each other all the time, or used to. It's not so common anymore. Mates that is." He chewed on some pasta.

"So, it's not just the fact that we're mates that I love to watch you eat. And sleep. And brush your teeth." I looked up as I started to tick off the things I loved to watch him do. "Showering and cooking. Swimming. Oh, and definitely when you wrap your fist..."

"Don't! Or we'll never get off this island." He gave me a wink and I felt heat rise in my cheeks. Was that a blush? Was I fucking blushing?

The mortification was short-lived but lasted long enough to know the old me wasn't totally dead. Whew! I'd dreaded going back to work with this softness I'd developed.

We cleaned up and packed, and before I knew it, we were in the air, Aleric's wings flexing when the currents failed to carry us along. Dragon flight was much like bird flight, flapping to stay up when there were too few or weak air currents, and drifting peacefully when there were good currents. I huddled in the middle of his shoulder blades, bags around me like cushions.

I'd wanted one more night of sex with him in the glorious bed, or under the moonlight, but it wasn't meant to be. Not right now anyway.

I didn't know why I kept thinking this was the end of our relationship, because it wasn't. It would carry on, we just wouldn't be together every hour of the day. I found I'd come to enjoy knowing he was with me. I felt safe, like I didn't always have to keep my guard up for threats because he shared the watch with me. I knew the moment he left me to go back to his own world, that I'd have those shields up again.

I was always tense before Aleric truly became my

mate. As soon as we'd mated, I knew I could rest easy for a little while.

Maybe that was the problem now. I'd come to rely on him as a kind of backup. I didn't have to be on the alert every moment of my day.

I curled into myself, a bag of clothes under my head. I stroked the thick hide of his skin. Black flecked with blue. My dragon, my heart. I thought about the things we'd done, the words we'd said, and knew that life was not going to be the same. Sometimes I'd get to have peace, and at others I wouldn't.

We hadn't talked about the future, not a real future where we'd live together. We'd only agreed to see each other when we could. For a woman who'd been so afraid of losing herself, I hadn't put up much fight, when it came down to it, I thought with a smirk. Two months ago I'd barely let him anywhere near me. Now, I didn't want to face the fact he'd be back in his own world shortly.

The sky turned dark as we flew in the direction I guessed was home. I'd fallen asleep on the last two flights I'd taken with Aleric. This time, I wasn't exhausted from fighting myself, and the fear of being so high didn't grip me as badly. I was safe, no matter how high Aleric took me. I know that for a fact.

I couldn't see much, Aleric was far too wide, and as the sky turned dark. All I could see was the stars. I sprawled out and looked up. I'd never been so close to them before. I'd flown, but it was hard to see above yourself in a plane. Here, on Aleric's dragon back, I could see the balls of light closer than ever, but they were still so far away. Like the future I'd begun to dream about, they were out of reach. I'd never wanted a family or a husband and a house. Not really. Aleric had changed that, and I was afraid it might never happen. The feeling of doom only grew the closer we got to my home.

10

*A*leric landed in a dark spot in the parking lot of my apartment building. He shifted to his human form as soon as I was off his back and the bags fell to the ground. A mosquito immediately bit me on the arm, and another tried to land on my cheek. I flailed around for a minute, and the tiny little bastards flew off. Aleric laughed and I gave him the finger.

"It's not funny when it's you they bite," I told him. I still had on my island attire: a dress that barely protected me from the chill of the air, much less from the last few mosquitoes of the season that were immune to the cold.

"Nah, they don't bite me. They hate dragon blood. If any are stupid enough to bite us, they just go poof, in a tiny little cloud of smoke." He grinned at me and hugged me close to his chest. "I'd come up, but I'll never leave if

I do. I should get back home. Can you handle your bags?"

I looked around, there were only two, and I'd have no problem taking those in. "Yeah, I can handle it. I'll miss you, Aleric. I didn't think I'd ever say that, but I have because I will."

It was about as romantic as I'd get.

"I will ache for you with every moment we are apart, Edana. And I will not be gone from you a single second longer than I have to be." He swept me up to his lips then, and kissed me with a passion that I knew was meant to cement the feel of his lips pressed on mine straight into my brain. And it did.

Oh, how it did. I clung to him in a way I would have never thought possible, my fingers all but clawed into his arms. Why did this have to end? Why was I so afraid of being away from him? The words "don't go" were poised on the tip of my tongue, but he shifted and flew away before I could say anything. He'd even managed to snatch up the bags in his claws in the process.

I knew it was the best way, the easiest way, but it still hurt to know he was going away from me and that he hadn't lingered. Rip that band-aid off as quickly as possible and get the pain over with. It was a decision I couldn't help but admire.

I picked up the bags and walked to the lit area of my building. Tonight, I was grateful there was an elevator.

Normally, I didn't use it because I preferred the exercise of the stairs, but with the bags in my hands, and heartache bending my shoulders, I'd decided to take the elevator.

I'd known heartache in my life, when my mother and grandmother died. I'd felt it keenly. It wasn't a new emotion to me, nor was love. Familial love was something I knew well. I'd loved my cousins when we were all younger and still did. I'd just distanced myself from them over the years. It was part of my job, mainly because it was easier to hide what I did if nobody talked to me. Romantic love, passionate love, that was totally new and because of it, this heartache felt somehow worse than when I'd lost my mother and grandmother.

I felt the pull of the bags, though they barely weighed anything between my shoulder blades and my head slumped down. That's probably why I didn't notice the man at the door.

"Edana." He spoke my name softly, with hesitation, but it was familiar. A voice I hadn't heard in a very long time. This was a voice that made me pause.

"No." My head lifted, but I didn't turn to look at him. "You don't get to be here now. You don't get to invade my life with your bullshit. Go back to wherever you were."

I pushed open the door, but he put his hand on the

back of my shoulder. I turned, a vicious hiss escaped my lips, and anger rose within me.

"What part of no did you not understand?" I felt a new power well up within me. Something I'd never felt before and I wondered if my eyes glowed, it felt as if they did.

"I've been looking for you, Edana..." he said with sadness in his voice. "Please, just give me..."

"No, I told you. Go back where you came from." So this is who had been plaguing Arista. Not my boss. "And leave Arista alone. You aren't my father anymore. You lost the privilege the day you left without a word. Now, piss off."

"Edana. You're in danger." It was a desperate bid to keep my attention, and it worked. Only not for the reason he wanted.

"I've been in danger since the day you left me alone. I've fended for myself this long, why do you think I need you now?"

"Because you're a part of me. And all the shifter world is in danger now." He had the grace to look away from me. "I'm not just trying to take advantage, Edana. There really are things I need to tell you."

"I don't think so." I turned away. This man might be my father, but he was a stranger. A stranger who'd showed up when I'd finally found some happiness in the world, like a leech there to suck all of the joy away. As he'd always done.

"Aleric will die if you don't listen to me." His words were spoken with haste, as if in a last-ditch effort to make me hear him.

I bit my lip, but not in indecision. I wanted to scream in anger, in frustration. This, *this*, was why I hadn't wanted to have a mate. He was a weakness that could be used against me now.

"How do you know who Aleric is?" I would kill whoever the spy was who'd revealed that, I decided, and made a gesture for him to follow me. I'd kill him if it was necessary. I had no illusions about the man, he'd abandoned me once already, after all.

"Thank you. I'll explain when we have some privacy." I headed for the elevator, keys in my hand. They'd been in my pocket when Aleric flew off with me. I always kept my keys there. Just in case I needed to get into my apartment quickly. You learned things like that in my line of work.

I pushed open the unlocked door a few moments later, and let my father into my apartment. It wasn't a lot, the basic necessities of life with a living room, bedroom, kitchen, and bathroom. I didn't spend a lot of time here so there were no plants, no pets of any kind unless you counted the spiders that often took up residence on my long absences. There were no family photos or mementos of past travels. Just the basics of life. My office at work held the only pictures I'd kept from my old life. A photo of Arista and Willow as children.

I flicked the lights on, dropped the bags on the floor beside the door, and went to pour a shot or two of bourbon in a glass on the cheap divider that made the living room and kitchen separate rooms.

"Right, you have five minutes." I stood there, my face scrunched with a glare. I didn't offer him a drink, I just waited. He wasn't about to get hospitality from me.

"I had to leave, Edana. I'd put you all in danger. I need more than five minutes," he pleaded, hands out to implore me to give him more chance.

I stared coldly at the man who was supposed to teach me to ride a bike and to drive a car, the man who was supposed to be there to warn my first boyfriend about guns and violence if he hurt me. He hadn't been around for any of that. I'd learned to ride a bike on my own because he'd been too drunk to teach me. My aunts taught me to drive. I'd dealt with the first man I'd slept with on my own. "You have four left."

He scraped a hand over his unshaven jaw, a week's growth from the looks of it. "Look, Edana, there are things you don't know, secrets you haven't been told. And not is all as it appears in Aleric's world."

"Pardon?" I sat down on the cheap brown couch I

sometimes fell asleep on because it was closer than the bed. Some nights, I'd come home too exhausted to do more than get inside the door before I sat down. I studied my father.

He'd barely aged. There were hints of lines to come around his eyes, a strand or two of silver in his hair at his temples, but otherwise, he'd barely changed at all. I could see my own eyes in his, and that angered me. I didn't want to look like him at all.

"What are you now, fifty-six? And you're still skulking in the shadows after all of this time?" I wondered how he'd managed in a nest of dragon slayers. He answered me with his next sentence, though I hadn't spoken out loud.

"I ran from my home world, Aleric's world, a long time ago, Edana. I needed to hide, and your mother's home was the best place to do that in. I used a gem to mask the fact that I was a dragon, but your mother's family. Well, most of them were hostile to me anyway. I thought the last place my enemies would look for me was in a slayer enclave."

I rolled my eyes, pursed my lips, and took a sip of the warm bourbon. It burned a trail down my throat that bloomed in my chest as I watched him. "So you were running from fate even then, were you?"

"There were things happening, Edana. Things in my world that still haven't been revealed." His hand went up to scrape through hair that should be completely white by now, but his dragon nature had slowed the aging process. Even mine was slower than most and I could pass for my mid-20s if I wanted to.

"Well, that's helpful. It wasn't nice to see you again, and it's time for you to go." I pointed at the door as I took another sip of my drink.

I wanted to scream at him, to make him tell me why he'd left me when I was just a defenseless little girl, but I also didn't want to hear excuses. They'd probably be lies.

"Edana, I would have died if I hadn't left, and so would you." His words came out with an air of defeat. "You may yet die if you don't listen to me."

"We're never guaranteed another day. Mom taught me that." My words were cruel, but they were meant to be. They were spoken to cause even a little bit of the sting I'd felt for all of these years.

"Look, you and your sister..." He went quiet when I broke in.

"I don't have a sister, Thad. There was only me, or did you forget that?" There we go, more of the bullshit. He couldn't even keep how many kids he had straight.

"What? No, Willow, who else would I mean?" He looked at me with confusion as I felt the world narrow down to a pinpoint that included only him, only his face. Willow...?

"Willow is my cousin, Thad. She isn't my sister." I felt

my pulse race as the world lost focus and panic settled into my chest. It couldn't be true... could it?

"No, didn't Rachel tell you? Willow is your sister." He stared at me with bewilderment. "That's why I left. Her sisters found out we were involved and they raised hell."

"Willow is my sister?" There was a strange pressure between my ears, and I could barely hear myself speak.

"That wasn't the only reason. James's men had found me..." His words trailed off as if he'd only just realized I wasn't really paying attention.

"Who is James?"

"The leader, well, former leader of the Mungon clan. The Alexander's took care of him."

I put a hand to my chest, a miserable attempt to slow down my heart. Willow was my sister and Rachel hadn't told me? All those years and she hadn't said a word? Did Willow know?

Pictures of Willow as a child flitted through my mind, the way I'd adored her from the first moment she'd been born. The way I'd cared for her, even when I could barely care for myself when I was a teenager. And I'd left her behind, to keep her from the influence of my coldness, my careless approach to the world. I'd become reckless at 15, started to do things I shouldn't. A year later I'd begun to sleep with men I shouldn't, and I'd seen the censure in the eyes of those in my community. I'd left to spare her from all of that.

And to seek a place where I belonged.

"Why didn't Rachel tell us we were siblings?" I asked.

"She was ashamed of our relationship, that's probably why. Your mother loved me, but she wasn't my mate. I loved her. When I lost her, it hurt, and Rachel gave me comfort. I think she was just lonely because there was no love there. It was just... physical. I think, in a way, it was how she rebelled against her own mother. It was the way she chose to make her mark on the world. They couldn't sense I was a dragon, but they still didn't like me. When James found me there, a man I don't wish on my worst enemy, by the way, I left to keep you all safe. He'd follow me, focus on me, and leave you all alone."

I watched him, gray eyes cold now and I felt no warmth emanating from them at all. The glow had gone.

"She never did say who Willow's father was. I guess that's why." I paused, my brain started a dull thud, and I wanted to just go to sleep. "So what made you decide to come in and pollute my world then, Thad? You haven't fucked it all up enough, you need to add more to it?"

"I'm sorry, Edana. I hadn't planned to come to you, I'd planned to leave you alone and to not draw attention to you. But you're mated to the offspring of the devil. Almost literally. I thought you deserved to know."

The world narrowed again.

11

In our time together, locked away from the world, Aleric and I had discussed very little about the problems we faced. I knew he was an ally, but the group that I worked for, that I was a part of, was not a group that I could talk a lot about. I knew more about his family affairs than he knew about my life, and that had often made me wonder if he actually loved me or if it was the mating bond that drove his adoration of me.

My father was gone, and right now I wanted nothing more than to have Aleric near me, to erase the world with his hands and his mouth, to make the world go totally blank for me. I went to sleep and I slept for two days. I woke up long enough to eat, do what I needed to do to keep my body from waking me up with painful demands, and went back to sleep.

By the third day, mother nature had pissed off. I felt awake, and I was kind of prepared to face the rest of the world. Kind of. At least mother nature didn't mess around with me for as long as I've heard some women have to face. I don't know if it's my dragon side or just my biology, but I've always been lucky as far as that goes.

I stretched as I waited for the water to get hot over the sink in my bathroom. It was a small room that contained a bath/shower, a toilet, and the sink. Laundry facilities were downstairs in the basement. Which was probably a good thing, because I doubted the tiny apartment could hold much else besides a laundry hamper. And a very small one at that.

I felt a buzz in the back of my brain and sighed happily. I let a connection open, a small mental window, and heard Aleric sigh in my head. "I've missed you."

"Did you? I thought you'd be glad to be shut of me for a little while. How are you? I've noticed you've slept a lot."

"I thought I felt you trying to buzz me a time or two." I smiled as I wiped a hot washcloth over my face and scrubbed away two days of sleep. The heat felt good and I let the wet cloth rest between my eyes. "God, that feels good."

"I know what would feel better." I heard his voice as

a sultry softness as an image flooded my mind. Aleric between my thighs, his tongue softly licking at my center as his hand grasped at my hip possessively.

My knees went weak and I sat down on the edge of the tub. "Oh, don't do that to me. I need to get to the office. Or find food. Something."

Luckily, my job wasn't one of those nine-to-five kind of deals; it was show up at odd hours and nobody would bat an eyelid kind of job. I could walk back in and pick right up where I left off, although, my boss would have noted my absence. After all the years I'd been there and not taken a vacation, I didn't expect anything more than concern.

"Oh, you aren't going to leave me with this are you?"

A soft kind of touch made me aware of the mechanisms that made vision possible in my eyes; I could feel it on the nerves and in the orbits. That touch turned into sight, but not my own. I glanced down, though I hadn't meant to, and saw exactly what Aleric was looking at.

"What have you been thinking about then?" I asked as a grin spread over my face as I sank down to the floor. I meant it as a tease, a way to segue into dirtier questions, but he took the conversation to a whole other level.

"The first time I had you." His words were ragged

and I felt a throb down there. But not *my* down there
—*his* down there. I didn't move but I felt him move to
grasp himself. There was a moment of awareness, sensation, before the loose grip and the subtle movements
blossomed into pleasure. "It was so good, Edana. I relive
it now that I'm here alone. I play it over and over in my
head when I have to deal with my father's tantrums
about how long I was gone, or when he doesn't like
something that's been brought to his attention. I relive it
when I'm in my chambers at night, in a cold, empty bed.
I can't get you… fuck, I can't get you off my mind."

The last words came out on a groan as he stroked the
hard length of his erection. I felt it, as if it were my own,
and shivered with him when the pleasure made his toes
curl. I let him lead my thoughts, give me the images he
thought of. Through his eyes, I felt truly beautiful for
the first time in my life. I'd never seen myself the way he
saw me, the way his eyes focused on mine when I cried
out his name. I'd never seen the way I moved as a beautiful dancer until I saw how he adored watching me
when I came. His images and memories shifted around,
from beginning to end, to the middle, to the part where
he watched me just before I came apart in a million
pieces.

I shuddered through those moments with him, as he
built himself to a buzz that ran along his spine. He
stopped suddenly, and my head filled with my name.

"I can't take much more of this, Edana. Can I come to you? I need to feel you beneath me." His words were ragged again, almost a groan of need.

I was too fascinated with what he was doing, of feeling like I had one of *those* of my own. It was a unique experience that I didn't want to end. I'd always wondered what it felt like for men, if it felt anything similar to what a woman felt. I'd heard the male orgasm only lasted a split second, that it wasn't nearly as long or complex as the female orgasm. I wanted to know if it did, if they felt that same build up of pleasure that could change, become so much more, and then explode into a something that could make you scream so loud you woke up the neighbors.

"Don't stop, Aleric. Carry on. Please. Let me watch, let me feel this."

"What?" he asked, confused, but he took his cock back in his hand without protest. I felt it again, that tight pulse as blood surged through his body, into the hardest part of him. I felt my body as it moved, spread out on a white rug on the floor, but I didn't really feel the movement or plan it. I just sprawled there, somehow not there, because I *was* Aleric just then.

"This, my love. The way it feels when you masturbate. It's so good. No wonder you men are always trying to give it attention."

"Does it feel like this for women?" he panted, not

distracted at all as he focused on what he was doing. He knew what was happening, and it made him just a little bit cocky when he answered. I heard the smirk in his voice, felt it on his face as if it was my own.

"Kind of. It's... different. I'll show you. Later." I thought about it, he thought about, how it would feel for him to be me, to watch me, to experience my feelings as I came. The way I was experiencing him now.

"Watch this," he prompted, and I looked down, at his cock, my cock for a moment, and we both grinned together. The head was full of blood; it throbbed with it. I thought it couldn't get any more swollen with need. Then it did. "That's because I thought about the taste of you on my tongue."

As Aleric spoke the image filtered into my brain, a small time delay that didn't change the way I tasted, the way he tasted me, or the way it made his gut go tight and his cock get just a bit harder.

It was all a bit odd, but that didn't change the fact it was one of the most erotic things I've ever experienced. To be in somebody's body, to feel what they felt and experienced, while still separate, was incredibly mind-blowing.

"Edana. Watch, baby. Don't think. Just feel it with me." Something had changed. Something tightened inside of him somewhere, and my breath caught in my chest.

His hand moved faster, and I began to breathe again, only now it was a pant as his fingers flew in a loose grip that seemed perfect somehow. I'd always thought it was best to grip a man tight, so he could feel it, and I'd never really taken the time to watch how they touched themselves. I'd just done whatever I wanted to do, and got my own before I moved on. Aleric had taught me there was far more to sex than just getting off.

There was sharing pleasure and giving pleasure. Getting pleasure through the giving. It was a whole new world that wasn't just a matter of dragon and human world. This was a world of lover and lover, not man and woman or human and dragon. I felt my knees go tight, and something between my legs grew tighter, and I couldn't breathe. It was gasp after gasp as my real toes curled and the sensations became so much more than intense.

I waited, I needed, whatever it was that was about to happen, I wanted it. I wanted to say something, do something that would push him over, that would end that incredibly erotic but painful sensation of constriction that filled Aleric. His thoughts flew, the images flitted in my mind, and then he settled on one. My mouth wrapped around him, my eyes on his as I came with him in my mouth. Only, I saw it, felt it from his perspective, and even though I hadn't touched myself, some spark flew from my clit to my inner walls, and I felt the first pulse of his orgasm as my own.

I pulsed with him and felt the incredible relief as he emptied out in waves that felt like thick jets of relief. It went on, nothing like the entwined completion that we usually found together, but still a moment that we shared, that we both felt. We were connected in that moment, maybe even more than we entered the dragon world together.

I panted in the floor, my head quiet, my heart pounding. Aleric tried to speak, he tried to form thoughts, but his brain was empty. Mine wasn't much better, but it didn't last long. How to describe that? What did I say?

"You want to come over?" I sat up, braced on my elbows and stared not at my own walls, but at the stone walls of Aleric's quarters. His chambers.

"You know I do. I just need to take care of something first." Our worlds were on different times, and I finally gathered enough wits to look at the clock in my living room. Over the television, I'd placed an old clock I'd found in a second-hand store. It was old, clunky, made of pine, and did not suit the rest of the cheap interior I'd installed in the place, but something about it reminded me of home and I'd been unable to leave the shop without it.

"I"ll be waiting for you." My boss could wait another day, I decided. I needed to feel the wild surge of Aleric's hips between my thighs, the silky wall of his back as I dragged my fingernails down the length. I needed to hear him groan my name as he came.

The world could wait for one more day. I didn't care if anybody like it or not. I needed one more day with my mate.

It would take him an hour to get here, so I headed back into the bathroom. I prepared myself for his touch and soaked away my cares. For the first time in my life, I was being truly selfish. Yeah, I was a bit selfish with men in my past, but they got what they wanted and so did I, it was an even exchange. I'd never taken *time* for myself, not like this.

When he arrived there was no talking. You'd think we'd been apart for months the way we came together in one resounding clench. Instantly, hands began to move, clothes flew away, and we were naked, pressed together on the floor because my couch was too small to hold his tall frame. I didn't care, not when he had my hands pinned over my head with one fist while his mouth teased a nipple to a tight point. His other hand was between my thighs, but he didn't move it.

He teased me with the promise of what was to come while his tongue drove me nearly to insanity. My nipples were sensitive, and Aleric had proven more than once that he could set me off with just his tongue there.

"You can't do this to me, Aleric, I need to feel you

inside of me." The words came out as a pant, and he made a sound of agreement, but didn't move.

I had zero control, none, and I loved it. Only Aleric could do this, only Aleric could take my control from me. No man was ever good enough to give myself up to like that.

I inhaled his scent: woods, smoke, and his own pheromones. It made my head swim, but I held on. Totally helpless, I waited to see what he'd do. What he wanted to extract from me today.

"You know you're the only man I'd trust like this don't you? I'd have caved in his chest and kicked him out of my door before I let him pin me to the floor like this?" I needed to say something, anything, to break my concentration. I wanted to last, not come like a school-girl with her first blush at being touched.

"I guess that's good because I'd cave in any man's chest that tried this with you, too." He let my nipple go long enough so he could speak. His head swayed to the other one, and he gave it one long lick before he caught it with his teeth.

A twang of sensation shot down my abdomen, straight to my center where it bloomed as one deep throb.

"This isn't going to be quick is it?" I asked with a smirk and he shook his head. That had the added effect of making his teeth twist my nipple and my hips shot up to grind into his. It was sweet pain that I only wanted from him.

12

*I* felt a flutter deep in my abdomen and a sensation of being full as he tugged at my nipple with his lips. He was braced over me, his strength on display, and I wanted to touch him, to feel that strength. I tugged at his hand to try to break his grip, but he only tightened the restraint.

"Stay still." An order. Oh my.

I grinned, despite the moment, and settled in for whatever Aleric had planned.

His hand twitched between my thighs, and I gasped. My hands clenched around his as a reflex, and my hips surged up.

I heard a low rumble and realized Aleric was pleased with my desperate response. Was he going to torture my nipples until I flew apart or was he going to give me what I really wanted? That hard length of pure bliss he saved just for me?

His hand moved, grazed my inner thigh, and I jumped. My thoughts were only on him now, I couldn't distract myself anymore. His hand ran down my thigh, and back up the other one. When he came close to my center, I twisted to capture his hand, to make the contact come quickly, but he didn't stop. His hand moved up higher over my ribs, until he clenched my other nipple. When he pinched it tightly, I couldn't resist anymore and my will melted entirely.

I had no shame as I clenched my thighs around him, around where he pressed into me, his cock hard between my inner folds. I twisted and found out the tip of his length buzzed right over my clit. With need a frantic ache inside of me, I moved as he tortured my nipples, both of them. Pants followed by a deep breath, and then I flew into the darkness.

I felt completely lost, totally exposed, totally out of control, but I didn't care, because Aleric had me. Aleric would keep me safe. Aleric would give me exactly what I needed. I didn't care, because I did care... about him.

He didn't stop his attention when my body came back to the ground, oh no; he slid into me then, a long, slow glide that stretched me out gently. I felt every centimeter of his girth, and then his length as he slid inside like I'd prepared a pot of warm honey just to home him in.

When he'd sunk down into me as far as he could go, he pressed a thumb to my clit. My hips bucked away, the touch was too much, but he didn't stop.

"Stop fighting me, Edana," he grunted as he began to grind into me softly. "Let me show you just how much you can take, baby."

I could only pant a response, I couldn't even form words. My hands were still over my head as Aleric fucked me, still totally his, and I watched his face.

His control was on the edge. He'd slip if I pushed. I didn't want that though. I wanted him to have whatever he wanted to take. Right now, that was all I had to give him, and I'd give it gladly.

His thumb pressed deeper into my clit, and I couldn't help but follow his lead. We moved in time together, and it was perfect. It was far more intense than that first climb to release. This race to the finish was hotter, harder, and so much more because he was inside of me, a part of me, and I felt my dragon come out to play.

My eyes closed, and in my mind, I saw Aleric's dragon reach out and entwine around me until we merged. Pleasure rocked through me. My nails clawed into his hand, and my spine bent backward as bone-breaking waves of ecstasy shot up from where we were joined to my brain. This was what I'd missed, this moment when we were complete. Even more than the pleasure, this fusion of our dragon souls satisfied a need deep inside of me.

The world was flames once more, and we were one. We soared together, a sensation of flight, without leaving the floor. We went into the heavens, into the dark sky, and a new light flared. Bright white and hot, the light did not burn, but it washed away so much pain I'd felt without even realizing it.

This was the power of dragon fusion. We healed each other as we became each other.

When we fell back to the real world, my world, I found we were both panting and our hearts were racing. "I can't fucking breathe!"

"I know, I can't either." But we could, otherwise we wouldn't have air to speak. That wasn't the point, our hearts felt like they were going to explode.

"How is it possible not to die from this shit?" I asked, my hand over the area where my heart raced in my chest. It kind of hurt.

"I don't know, but I want to do that again. Soon."

He picked me up then and carried me into my bedroom. I pointed it out to him, pushed the door open, and he sat me down on the bed.

"You look tired, my love." A phrase I never thought

I'd say out loud to anyone, but it worked in the moment. He knelt at the side of the bed, his head on my stomach. I twined my fingers in his silky hair and waited for his answer.

"My father grows worse, and I'm the only one there to deal with it. Mary has her own tasks now that Malcolm and Henry have been banished. The workload has increased and she nearly lost her mind while I was gone, but now that I'm back, it's helped."

"What do you mean, worse?"

"He's sporadic, makes demands, and then changes his mind after we've done as he told us to. He had a man executed last week for using too much water on his fields, and then changed his mind. After the man had been beheaded."

"My God, Aleric! He has to be stopped!" I looked down at him with horror. His father had definitely gone around the bend then. "Is there anything you can do?"

"Not that I know of. He's ruler until death or abdication, whichever comes first. I fear some of the ministers are working to oust him and replace the monarchy with a different kind of government, but there's nothing I can do about them right now either. There are so many whispers, so many rumors, it's all maddening and difficult to find the truth. I don't want to tell Father about my suspicions because he'd have them all killed. It's chaos, pure chaos."

He sighed against my stomach, and I tugged at his hair. "Come up here. Cuddle with me."

I took him in my arms when he came up, his head against mine.

"That's not all. This plague of vampire blood is spreading. Between the crisis over the birth rates and this new drug, shifters are going stark raving mad. It's been hell trying to keep this under control."

"Have you got a police force?" I asked, a suggestion in mind.

"Yes, it's part of the military force. They're trying to keep the blood from coming in, but it's being trafficked in along with undeclared humans. Father agreed to honor the decree he set when Willow had control of his body and mind, but they still aren't following the rules."

"Yes, Willow told me about all of that. So, even though they can legally bring in partners now, they still aren't complying?"

"I think some are afraid their partners would try to run away. That is one thing Father did change in the decree. Any partner that tries to flee back to their own world will be executed. Maybe that's the problem?"

"It would be a huge problem for me. I can't promise I won't come back to my own world if I go to yours."

"You're different, though, Edana. You're a halfling, so you could come anyway, without any restrictions. These are humans, brought from your world and other worlds like it. They don't know about everything that happens in our world and when they're brought in, many panic and want to go back home. I can't say that I blame them right now."

He sighed and stroked a hand up my waist. "It's a problem I don't know how to fix."

"Maybe you'll have to... I don't know.. *force* your father to abdicate." I tiptoed around the word, but it was the one I meant.

"How can I do that? He's the king, I can't force him to do anything." He fell back against the pillows, his hand over his eyes to block it all out.

"Tell him you'll leave and not come back. You're his last heir. Force his hand." It sounded like a good plan to me.

"That might work. But then again, he might just get pissed off and tell me to leave. He's so unpredictable since he started taking this vampire blood. I can't place it, but there's something more wrong with him too, Edana. Something that makes my blood run cold."

"What's that?" I sat up and looked down at him. His blue eyes met mine, and I saw uncertainty there.

"I'm not sure. He just doesn't seem to be... himself. There's something not right about him. Sometimes, when I look at him, he goes a little fuzzy. Maybe that's my own eyes, maybe I need some of your human spectacles to clear that up?" He gave a self-deprecating laugh.

"No, that sound familiar, actually." Something buzzed in the back of my brain, but it wouldn't be teased out for any amount of money. I went through my memories: books I'd read, files I'd seen, mentions I'd heard, but it didn't come back to me. "Maybe it's the blood, maybe it's making him run at super speed?"

"It could be, I guess. In the Alexanders' world, your world, the drug makes shifters stronger. They're a different breed from us, they can shift into whatever they like, a spirit animal usually. I can only shift into a dragon. Maybe it will have a much different effect on my people?"

"It might, yeah. I don't know. It's crazy to even contemplate, shifters drinking vampire blood. Like those people are some kind of cow to be bled of their very... oh, wait. That's kind of how they treat humans, isn't it?"

"In the end, yes. They have volunteers that donate their blood to the vampires in your world. It's very underground, exclusive and secretive, but it exists. Vampires don't exist in my world. Only in yours, so it's all new to me, but Cade told me about it when I saw him at your cousin's house."

I went still then. "Um, actually..."

"What?" He turned his head to me when he heard my tone.

"It seems Willow is my half-sister. She's more slayer

than dragon though, so she doesn't even know she has a dragon side."

"Ah, that explains Marya's power then."

"You saw that pink flash too, huh?"

"Several times now. She's going to be a very strong dragon one day. Worthy of the crown, actually."

"I didn't know Willow was my sister. My father was here, the night that you brought me back. He dumped a load of shit on me. I listened to some of it, but then I made him go. He's a conman, probably looking for money and a place to crash, offering promises of secret information. I don't want him in my life."

"He's your father, though. What's his name again?"

"Thad," I said abruptly, and pushed up in the bed, a blanket over my nudity. "He left me when I was only a child. After he got Rachel pregnant and abandoned her, that is."

"Thad. I don't remember that name."

I glanced over to see Aleric was trying to remember him.

"He might be from a different world, though he did say he'd been from yours. He was probably banished, and that's why you don't know anything about him."

"Maybe so. He could have been one of my father's guards. There was a revolt, a month before I was born, but Father squashed it and we don't know a lot about it. It was forbidden to ever talk about it."

"Oh?" That was news to me. Interesting. "What do you know?"

"Only that. Some dragon guards tried to overthrow my father, and the rebellion was put down before it even began, really. There wasn't much ever said about it. I only know about it because I heard some bears talking about it when I was young. They disappeared, probably off in another world, bears roam a lot, so I never got to ask them about it."

"What a shame. It would be nice to know a little more about that." I slid back down in the bed, my hand twined in his. "Shall we lay all of this aside for a while and get back to what we're best at?"

I gave him a sultry look and he responded with a grin that nearly melted my blanket it was so sensually charged. "That sounds like a very good idea, Edana. The best we've had all night."

He pulled me beneath him and made me scream his name several times, loud enough that I'm sure I'd get complaints from my neighbors, but didn't care. He fell asleep in my bed while I showered.

When I came back in and saw him there, my past came back to me. For a moment, my brain asked why he was still in my bed. My heart answered that question quickly enough. Because I want him to be, it said.

I put on some silk short pajamas, and then slid into bed with him, my hair a wet curtain down my back. I ran a finger down his jawline, watched as it clenched and then relaxed. He felt as safe here with me as I did with him. It was a totally new experience, having a man in my bed. I'd slept with him in the cabin and then in the beach house, but this was new. He was not only in my apartment but in my bed. Where he belonged.

13

---

$\mathcal{I}$ walked into the basement level offices of Shinar, (ancient Sumerian for Land of the Watchers) and went straight to my own space. The floor was cloaked in darkness, and no bright lights were to be found. The faint lights from computer screens, office equipment, and small desk lamps were all that illuminated the interior, which was always cold, even in the winter. I kept my head down, unlocked my door, and scurried to my desk.

I was dressed in my usual black-on-black ensemble when at work, a reflection of the environment and also my mood at the moment. My hair was pulled up in a bun, and I wore very little makeup. I was here to work, not make friends or win admirers.

There was little I wanted to say to anyone anyway, not until I had my head around everything, and a report ready for Adony, my mentor in my early days with the secret agency, and now my boss. I pressed the button to start my desktop and waited for the program to load. I looked up when I saw movement, but the figure walked by without a pause. I felt like a thief who had stolen in to steal information, or something else nefarious. I wasn't, I'd just come to work, but still, I'd been away for so long, and had kept so much to myself, that it felt wrong to be back.

I sat back when I saw the emails in my inbox. Hundreds of them, from field agents, Adony, and some of my coworkers. These were the only people that knew my email address, I didn't want to think about what my personal email looked like. I sighed and chewed the corner of my thumb.

I'd been with this organization since Adony had found me as a young woman and promised me a life I could never dream of, with realities and truths that no longer had a place in human logic. As a dragon/slayer hybrid I'd offered a wealth of opportunity to Shinar to study and research. They also believed I would be an asset to the group, and I'd never let them down in that assumption. Until Aleric kidnapped me that is.

I stared at my computer screen, the report program open, the cursor a steady blink on the screen. What did I tell them? What did I keep to myself? All I could do was start to write and hope that some of it began to make sense somewhere along the way, because I was not going to tell them everything I learned, not in this report that would become a permanent record. I loved Aleric, I'd come to love him well beyond what our mating bond would produce.

There were things I did need to report though. Godwin's use of vampire blood, my thoughts about the vampires that had gone missing and where they might be located, and what had happened to them. I'd kept all of this from my thoughts in my time with Aleric mainly because I did not want to reveal who I worked for or that I suspected his father was kidnapping vampires.

There weren't many vampires left in my world, and even fewer were created now. In the old days, before citizen surveillance became a thing even democratic societies caved in to; when you didn't need a piece of government-issued paper for everything under the sun, vampires could proliferate with the increase in human population. Now, they had to hide in the shadows once more, and hope their wealth brought them an easier life. Not all vampires were rich, however, some had never had wealth, others had lost it. Those were the ones who had been reported missing.

It wasn't human interference either, from what I could tell. I tapped a finger lightly against my keyboard as I considered it all. Those who reported the missing vampires all said the missing one had been offered riches that they could not turn down. None of the informants could identify a person or group, because the vampire would get an email or text from the kidnapper. There would be a time and a place arranged, and the vampires would disappear afterward.

Fifteen vampires had gone missing before the head of the vampires in our world came to me. She was beautiful, seductive, and very deadly. 'Regal' defined the woman very well, which I suppose is proper for a woman who is a vampire queen in her own right, and queen of the magicals due to her marriage to Jacob Alexander. She'd come to me a week before Willow's daughter was born, a meeting that had taken place in secret. I couldn't even acknowledge I knew her when I went to Willow to see her child.

The meeting had been held in an abandoned warehouse, in an office that reeked of moldy, wet paper and neglect. I'd waited for her, wondering what could have prompted such a woman to contact me, when I didn't think anyone in the magical world really knew we existed anymore. The woman was over 600 years old, however, so I suppose it was no surprise, really.

She'd told me about the disappearance of over a dozen of her subjects in her sphere, and why she thought it was to do with this mysterious benefactor. The kidnapper had claimed to be with a company that tracked down recipients of inheritances that went unclaimed. Six had disappeared before anyone took any real notice, and then six more. By the time the last three disappeared, even Sabrina had known about.

An email I read earlier had revealed nine more had disappeared since my own disappearance. I doubt Sabrina had told my family about those disappearances or that I was looking into them because if she had, there'd have been even more of an uproar. No, my life was a web of secrets I had to work hard to keep untangled. My head ached. A lot.

I put my head in my hands now, squeezed in an attempt to ease the pain, and closed my eyes. This was not going to be easy. The Alexanders had been on my radar for a while, since Jacob was turned into a vampire and a king. A shifter vampire. The implications had been enormous, and when he became the king of the magicals of our world, everybody wanted to know more about him. Shinar had wanted to know more about him.

I hadn't known the queen herself would come to me, or that my family would become involved in the whole thing. When Arista had mated with a dragon shifter from another world, a whole new can of worms was opened. Now, I had a tangled mess that I was barely keeping apart.

I inhaled a deep breath, held it until I felt like my eyes had swollen and my chest might burst, and then slowly let it out. Calm...

That didn't help.

I had work to do, and somehow, I had to get all of this down. I opened a drawer of the metal desk and dug through files, papers, and books until I found a notepad. I had to dig around in the smaller drawer to find a pen. It was amazing how little we used such things now, when for generations paper and pens were so vital. It often made me wonder what would happen if all of the power went, and computers and servers became obsolete. How would we retrieve such a vast amount of information if some virus wiped out the world's data storage? It didn't bear thinking about so I started jotting notes on the yellow paper.

I started with my first meeting with Sabrina and worked my way down to the meeting with my father. By the time I'd finished, I'd gone through twenty pages, my hand was cramped, and four hours had passed. Somebody had brought in coffee and a sandwich, I remember reaching for them and having them there, but didn't remember requesting or receiving them. One of the staff who knew I was hot on the trail of something important, no doubt. That or my telekinesis was shaping up better than I thought.

I flipped through the pages, highlighted certain paragraphs, put stars next to sentences I didn't want to include, and started a new set of notes on another notepad. I copied the notes I wanted to keep to the new notepad, and then tore up the old ones. I tossed them into a metal wastebasket and flicked my finger. The paper inside the basket turned to flames, and when it was done, even the ashes were gone. A small trick that I very rarely used, but I didn't want anyone to see those notes. Only Adony knew about that talent, mainly because he'd taught it to me. I wasn't very much of a dragon, even the mating with Aleric hadn't changed that, but Adony had insisted I had enough in me to have skills. I hadn't been able to shift, and he often said he thought I held myself back from it. That I was afraid of it, but he could never coddle it out of me. Flames from my fingertips, sure, but shifting? Nope, nothing had ever worked. I hadn't even got into that halfway position that some shifters managed before they popped back into their human form.

I was a failure as a dragon, and an even worse dragon hunter, but as an investigator? I slayed!

My psychic abilities, the telekinesis, and the pyrokinesis might be considered some rather awesome weapons, but they didn't compare to the ability to turn into an animal at whim or shoot flames from your mouth. Now that I was back in touch with my family, I'd learned that Willow and Arista had their own unique powers and we could all communicate through some kind of psychic connection. I'm sure Adony had explained it all to me at some point, but I am also sure I probably tuned out the explanation.

The man was well over two thousand years old, though he barely look a day over fifty, even with that shock of white hair, and sometimes he forgot what he'd explained and what he hadn't. As a result, sometimes he explained things more than once, just to be sure. I'd learned to tune him out over time, which wasn't always a good thing.

I loved the man like a surrogate father. He'd brought me into Shinar, he'd given me a place, a home, and paid me very well to do my job, but sometimes, he could drone on. I wasn't always the best student, but I was a good investigator. I'd learned quite a bit about the Alexanders before Sabrina came to me, or my family brought them into an even closer range.

I could see now I needed to do three reports. One on the disappearance of Sabrina's vampires, one on my kidnapping, which would be brief, and one on the dragon shifters. Hmmm, no four. I needed to do one on the Alexander brothers as well. I turned to my computer and started to type.

So far, I hadn't learned a lot about what had happened with Sabrina's vampires, although I did suspect Godwin had more than a little bit to do with that. A king would not want to keep going through middlemen for the supply of his drug of choice. Especially when you could have that drug direct from the source. Some of the things Aleric had said would stay out of my report, but I would include the erratic behavior of the dragon king in my dragon shifter report. And in the Sabrina report, I decided. This would let my boss know I suspected a link.

I hurried through the reports on the shifters of both worlds and started on the report about my kidnapping. I kept that one simple and to the point. Aleric of Godwin, next in line for the throne, was my mate. I deleted that line twice, rewrote it, then deleted it again. Did I want Adony to know? Would I be able to keep that information from him? It had been difficult to hide the relationship from Adony in the weeks before Aleric took me. I didn't like to keep things from him, but this was something that could change my entire life. I'd kept it to myself. Could I go on?

I decided it was better to have that one strand in the web untangled and wrote the sentence out again. I added how I'd stayed of my own free will after I woke up, and that I did not want to take any kind of revenge against Aleric for taking me. He was my mate, that was all that needed to be known, really. Or, all I wanted to reveal, actually.

For now, I decided to play it cagey and leave out what I thought would be important for my investigation. We investigators were allowed this freedom because our bosses knew we'd been taught the best practices. Sometimes too little information could lead to wrong conclusions. It was best to wait until a fuller picture was revealed to make judgments.

That, and it was all so new to me. I couldn't wrap my own head around it, I didn't expect anybody else to be able to either.

I sat back and doodled on the notepad for a moment. A circle with lines beaming out from all sides. Godwin was in the middle of the circle, his world. From it sprang the missing vampires, which led to another thread with the Alexanders in place. Around those spokes, more lines revealed themselves, the shifter communities that were running out of mates, the shifters in Aleric's world that were now taking human mates. It all began to tangle together, but still, there was Godwin at the center of it all.

Jacob and Sabrina were now the king and queen of my world, of the magical world, but there was still entities above even them. The rulers of the realms, alien-like creatures who spoke with only one voice at the same time. They were almost divine entities, pale, tall, and an odd shade of white. Their color did not change, from their colorless eyes to their lips. Sabrina had mentioned them, and I knew about them, but I'd never seen them in person.

Nobody knew if they were shifters or vampires.

Some had speculated they were both, or maybe even fairies. Nobody knew and they weren't the kind to have polite conversations about 'what are you', with anybody. I had to wonder what they knew about all of this. They seemed to be omnipotent, yet they sometimes needed answers. Would I be able to meet with them, find out what they knew? As the rulers of all of the realms, with each king a kind of governor for each realm, they should know something about this, surely.

I looked through the directory on my computer, but found no way to contact them. I made a note to call Sabrina and update her. I'd also nudge my way into finding out how to contact them. If I was lucky.

# 14

"*He's* getting worse." Aleric's voice whispered into the folds of my brain, and somehow became a noise I could hear.

I was still at my desk, on the verge of taking the report to drop into the appropriate chute where it would be vacuum-suctioned to Adony's office. It was a system like those you might find at a bank's drive-through section. It proved efficient for carting around documents and other small objects and saved walking time for most of us.

The office actually had another level above and below the floor where my office was, I just rarely went to either. Adony's office was on the floor above mine, and below, well, there were cells down there for the really bad creatures that needed to be kept from all of the realms. The dark space, where sounds seemed to disappear before they were even made, wasn't a place I went to often.

"I'm listening," I sent back and settled down into the chair. "Is it your father?"

"Yes. I need to contact my brothers and maybe even the Alexanders. I'll be at your place in an hour." His 'voice', the sound in my head at least, was strained, as if he was stressed, but didn't want to talk about it yet.

"I'll be there. Be careful." I'm not sure why I said that last part, he was a dragon, there wasn't much that could hurt him. I felt the need to, though, so I did.

I picked up the papers, my bag, and jacket, and went to the bank of chutes. I placed the file in a tube, stuck the tube back in the chute, and it whooshed off to Adony's office. I still hadn't spoken with him, but Aleric needed me.

On the drive home, I pinged Arista and Willow in my head, and they agreed to come to my place. I'd never had guests at my house. Well, the occasional one-night stand didn't count, did it? I stopped at the grocery store, bought some drinks, snacks, and a candle or two to make the place look less... depressing. I even picked up a cheerful tablecloth and some new glasses that were on sale. I'd never really cared about what my place looked like, as long as I had what I needed. I didn't want to look like a complete drudge to my family, however, so I made a small effort.

When I got home, I lit several of the candles, put one in the tiny living room, one on the counter in the tiny kitchen area, and one in the bathroom. I spread out the tablecloth, arranged vegetables onto a tray, stuck out some dip, and loaded another plate up with sandwiches. The glasses were washed and dried by the time Aleric knocked on my door.

He looked ragged, worn out. Time was fairly constant between our two worlds, and it had only been a day since I saw him, but it looked as if it had been months. He was thinner, his strong cheekbones stood out, and his eyes looked haunted.

"Aleric! What the hell has happened to you?" I cried out as I tucked myself under his arm and helped him to the couch. He sank into the hard cushions and I promised myself I'd get a new one the next day.

"I'll wait until the others arrive to tell you." He leaned his head back against the couch and sighed deeply. "I don't want to tell this story more than once."

I went to the bathroom to wet a washcloth with hot water and wiped his face down with it. He was covered in dirt, as was the black uniform and black leather tactical boots he wore. I could see that he was exhausted so I went to the kitchen, filled a bowl with hot water, and came back. I bathed his face again, his hands, his neck, and treated the cut I found on his right bicep. It was a deep gash, about three inches long. I wanted to ask about it, ask him how he'd got into this shape once more, but he'd said all he was about to say.

I went into the kitchen, emptied the bowl, and came back with a glass of iced tea. The real stuff, not that kind you pour out of jug from the store. It was my one take-away from my old life, the ability to make tea. He chugged down the first glass, so I went to get him another. When I brought him the glass back, there was a knock at the door.

"Hi, we're here," Arista said when I opened the door. She, Malcolm, Willow, Henry, and the babies Galen and Marya, all stood in my hallway. The men were both dressed in similar black attire, the habit a hard one to break I had to assume. Willow wore a long, black dress and a denim jacket, while Arista had on skinny jeans and a thick beige sweater that curled up in a cowl just under her chin.

"Hey. Thank you for coming. He's here already." I let them in, sat them where I could on my meager furnishings, and brought a chair in from the kitchen for me to sit on.

Malcolm and Henry sat with Aleric, both checking him over, and Willow and Arista sat on the coffee table. I didn't care; it was sturdy, but cheap. If it broke, I'd buy another one. "Do you two want chairs?"

"No, this is fine," Arista assured me, and I made a note to get better furniture. Maybe baby-proof the place. Both little ones were too small to wander right now, but that wouldn't last too long.

Both little ones were sleeping happily, and when Arista nudged Galen's car seat closer to Marya, their tiny hands drew together.

"Awwww!"

I couldn't help it, it actually popped out of my mouth. Arista smiled happily and looked at me with a pleased look. "They're going to be the best of friends."

"I think you're right," I mumbled and glanced at Willow. My sister. I hadn't seen her since I came back. Had she spoken with my father? Surely she'd have said something since I came back if she had.

My whole life she'd just been my little cousin, special to me, but my cousin. Now, she was my half-sister. And my cousin. Geez, my dad really had to go and make life weirder, didn't he? Why couldn't he have kept it in his pants? I wondered. But then, if he had, Willow wouldn't be there.

"Alright, that's enough. You two are like mother hens with a chick to share between them, get off of me!" Aleric pushed away from his brothers and glared at them. "I'll be fine. I'm just tired."

"What happened?" Malcolm demanded and Henry shook his head in support.

"There are a lot of secrets that need to be told. Eventually, we're going to have to bring in the Alexanders on this one, but right now, there are family secrets, secrets that we don't know we have. Some that we do, but haven't told." Aleric looked at me and I knew he meant my work.

"What are you talking about?" Henry asked. I didn't say anything, not yet. I wouldn't, not until I knew I needed to.

"Do you remember when father took us on that trip to the farmhouse? We had to chop wood, and cook on a wood-stove, heat water on the stove to bathe in? Do you remember that trip?" Aleric looked at his brothers in turn, and both nodded. "Do you remember *why* we went on that trip?"

"Father wanted us to have a taste of the real world," Malcolm said, but shook his head, as if that didn't make sense.

"Yes, it was to... build character after Mother passed away," Henry said, but even he didn't seem convinced now.

"Are you certain?"

"It seems fuzzy now," Mal mumbled, his right hand at his temple. "It was a long a time ago..."

"It was. I was only a small child, but I remember it. I also remember why we were there, exactly."

"What do you mean?" Henry prodded, his face suspicious.

"Father had taken us there to hide us all. We weren't

on a character-building trip. We were in hiding!" Aleric's voice stressed the last word and both of his brothers looked even more confused.

"Hiding? From what?"

"You two really don't remember?" Aleric asked, and then he looked resigned. "I guess it makes sense. I didn't remember until a couple of days ago. I've been gone for two weeks, Edana, in another land, where the time warps as it did with Arista and Malcolm in some of the worlds they've visited."

"Yeah, that part still makes my brain wobble," I said, but didn't say anything more.

"Who was he hiding us from?" Henry asked, and for the first time, I wondered where Mary was.

"Dagon." The name was familiar to me, but it didn't cause the reaction that it did in Henry and Malcolm. I remembered the name as some ancient fertility god, but nothing to be frightened.

"The Phoenician god of fertility?" Willow asked, and we all turned to her, surprised. "What? I read too, you know?"

"No, just that you know about him in this world. In our world, he is the thief of children, he takes them from one to give to another. Sometimes, well, sometimes he even..." Henry turned away and Malcolm finished for him.

"Sometimes, he eats the children. He is thought to be

the father of all vampires in our world. That the children he did not eat, were spread out to propagate the vampire lines."

"Oh." Both women snatched up their children, and even I felt a bit clingy at that point.

"And he was after all of you?" I prompted in an effort to get Aleric to continue.

"He wasn't after us, he was after father." Aleric paused, before he continued, his eyes on his hands. "He accomplished what he set out to do, as well."

"What? No, father is alive and well," Henry protested in disbelief.

"No, he's not." Aleric looked at both men before he continued. "Over the last few months, memories have been coming back to me in dreams. Sometimes I forget them soon after I wake up. I haven't been able to piece it all together. Last week, Father sent me to a new land, one I didn't even know existed, and there, I was taken prisoner."

I gasped and went to take his hand, but he sat back, away from us all.

"I was kept in the prison until I escaped. He wanted all of us gone. All of us but Mary. He plans to wed her."

"What the fuck, Aleric?" Malcolm burst from his seat and glared down at his brother. "Explain. Now!"

"Dagon killed Father's soul all those years ago and inhabited his body. His soul lives in Father's body, basi cally. Father is no longer in that shell. He left us a long time ago."

"Is that why he's using the vampire blood?" Arista popped up. "He's growing weak?"

"His poison has spread throughout the many realms, the many worlds, we all inhabit. There are other fertility gods, but the gods of your world, the Elders I believe you call them, Edana?" Aleric paused to ask. When I shook my head in agreement without meeting his eyes, he continued, "The Elders have decided it's time to end the plague that is Dagon. To do that, they've had to restrict the fertility of the shifters in all realms." That was met with more disbelief.

It was Willow who spoke first. "Why do that, though?"

"Without shifter children, the shifter world would be in an uproar. Their plan was to decrease the population, let the vampires increase so that they could battle the demon. Apparently, they are better equipped for it than we are." Aleric sighed. His hand was back at his forehead, and I knew he was in pain. He wouldn't ask for relief, yet, not until he was done.

"The elders are the reason we can't produce full-shifter children anymore. They didn't count on the vampire blood trade, or the fact that shifters would find human mates. They only wanted to end the plague that is Dagon, and the evil that spreads from him. He has polluted all of the worlds with his evil. Greed, drugs, abuse, it all boils down to Dagon in this world. In our world, it's the lack of children, the dying of our crops lately, the fact that so many are no longer happy. And it all comes down to Dagon."

"Then we'll call the vampires to help us. First, where is Mary?" Malcolm started but Aleric shook his head in defeat.

"We can't rely on the vampires. Dagon has been keeping dozens locked in our basements. He wasn't buying from the vampires of this world, he was supplying them! With their own kind's blood!"

"No, that can't be! Why else would Sabrina have come to me?" The words slipped out before I could stop them.

"Because she doesn't know. The Mungons were working with a faction that have left Sabrina's circle. They've been polluted by Dagon's greed and prey on their own now." Aleric paused. "Mary is locked in a tower. Once the wedding was announced, she, understandably, lost her mind. She tried to escape, and I'd been sent to the other world so I couldn't help. When I escaped and went back to our world, I found out. I tried to get her out, but I can't, not on my own. It's all a mess. I want to say our father has gone insane, but he hasn't, because that is not our father. Even if we killed the demon, father's soul is gone. Father is dead."

Aleric's words became a jumbled mess, and I really couldn't blame him. It was a lot to wrap your head around in a small amount of time.

All three men stopped speaking then, and I knew they were communicating with their minds. I didn't interrupt, I just sat there and waited. I had thoughts running through my own head, though. How do we defeat a demon? Would Adony still be at work? He definitely needed to know about this. He could help us.

"I'll call the Alexanders," Willow said and Arista pulled out her own phone. That seemed odd, but I guess they preferred it to mind-phoning. Mind texting? Mind emailing? Whatever, they used their phones instead.

"I'll make a call myself. Um, we might need to move this to one of your houses. I don't have any more room." I didn't want to break the moment, but I only had two chairs. The Alexander women would definitely need somewhere to sit and this place just wasn't up to their standards.

"That's fine, we can go to Willow's. Right Willow?" Arista turned to her cousin and Willow nodded happily. "Right then. We'll meet there in a half hour shall we?"

"You flew here?" I asked, with surprise. "It's still daylight!"

"We flew into the woods and landed, if anybody saw us, they wouldn't believe it. It seemed urgent so..."

Malcolm's voice trailed off. "I didn't know how urgent it was."

"I don't think any of us did. Let's go. I can make my call on the way." I grabbed my bag and phone, and we all walked out to the woods. The men shifted. We ladies and babies climbed aboard, and we were off. I had some explaining of my own to do, so I picked up my phone. First my boss, then my family. This was going to be a long night and there was still more to take in, on all sides.

15

"*D*agon is an old demon, Edana. You'll need more help than another shifter clan. You might need more than the vampires too. Even if you killed Godwin's body, my dear, you wouldn't kill Dagon. He'd likely just slay one your souls and take over that body." Adony sighed down the line and knew I probably should have brought my old mentor in on all of this a lot sooner.

"What can we do?" I asked, shame in my voice that I couldn't deny.

"I'll try to find something about him in the old scrolls. There may be something more we can do. I'll call you if I find anything.

I knew he meant mentally, if he couldn't get me on the phone, so I agreed and hung up. I felt terrible now that I'd called him and explained everything.

I'd thought I could handle it, I thought we were only dealing with vampire-blood addicted shifters. As usual, when it came to my life, nothing was simple. I looked across the sky and saw the other dragons in our group. One of those dragons was Henry, and on his back rested my sister. How was I going to explain the realities of our relationship to her?

I'd protected her when we were young, even when I could barely fend for myself. It was all a mess, and I'd yet to untangle it.

Despite the fact I could barely feel any wind protected in the cradle of space between Aleric's wings, my lips felt dry and I dug around in my bag for my lip moisturizer. My hand brushed against the box I'd left in there, and I pulled it out to examine it again. I'd almost forgotten the thing. Small enough to fit into my hand, the box opened as soon I put it in my palm. I'd spent many hours trying to decipher the language but it never stopped shifting around. I sighed, closed the lid, and put it back in my bag. That was for another time then.

We landed at Willow's and Henry's house with quiet flaps of the dragon's wings. The men shifted back to their human shapes, and I saw how handsome they all were. Each different, but all hard soldier princes. Aleric was the most handsome to me, his lips were fuller, softer, and his eyes kinder. But then, he was my poet-soldier, wasn't he?

Willow and Arista, both mothers now, were softer versions of me. Their hair was a light brown, much softer than the cold hard black of my own hair. Even their eyes, a light brown that bordered on golden, was softer than the steel gray of my eyes. Now that I paid attention, however, I could see that Willow's features and mine were similar. Our hair and eye colors were different, but our body shapes, but our cheekbones, the almond shape of our eyes, and the slim, upward tipped shape of small delicate noses, were exactly the same. These were not features we'd got from our mothers.

I sighed as Aleric followed his brothers into the house. He paused to look back at me. "Everything alright?"

"Yeah," I said with a soft smile. "I just need a minute. My brain is tired."

He came back to me, tilted my chin up to his face, and kissed me. "Take all the time you need, but if you need me, I'll be inside."

I clasped my hands around his face and kissed him high on the right cheek. "I..."

I didn't say it though. I stopped, caught by the expression of my words that was reflected in his eyes. "I know. Don't be long."

He walked away and I felt my lips twist into an ironic smile. I loved him and he loved me. We didn't have to say it, though I guess we would eventually. We just knew it, our dragons knew it, and that was all that mattered on that subject. I felt a cold shiver of fear of what might happen in our future go down my spine as he entered the house. It hadn't fully sunk in that we were about to deal with a demon, but as he walked in and Alexanders started to show up, one as a raven, one as an eagle, one as a dragon with a group of ladies on his back, and the other as a... duck... a *duck*. Now that distracted me.

They congregated in front of me, and the ladies climbed down from the dragon before he shifted into a rather handsome man dressed in black leather from head to toe that should look ridiculous by all rights, but on him, made him look like a rather sexy rock-star. Or a king.

The men were easy to recognize, all three were dark-haired except one, and all handsome; the Alexander brothers. All but Jacob dressed in black, tailored suits. The women were an incredibly beautiful mix of femininity. Damesha, with her darker skin and blue eyes, was gorgeous in a pair of black leggings and a sweater dress that matched her eyes, But so was Jacqui with her pale skin, pale hair, and pale eyes dressed in a pair of white jeans with a black sweater. Then there was Sabrina and Allana. Jacqui and Damesha were some kind of witches, I could sense that about them. Sabrina, of course, was a vampire, and loved gothic romance if you judged by her black lace and silk dress that was a steampunk queen's dream dress. And Allana, the shifter, in jeans, cowboy boots, and a black and green flannel shirt. All, strong, able, and the kind of women I'd want at my side for this.

"Hey," I said simply, as they all stood in front of me. I kind of felt awkward around so much female and male beauty, and I wished I didn't feel so old compared to them. Well, Sabrina was older than all of us, but she didn't look it at all.

"Hi, again, Edana. You look different." Sabrina came up to me, pressed her cheeks to each side of mine in a symbolic kiss, and stepped back to look me over. "You're mated?"

"Yes," I said with a chuckle. "To Aleric."

"Oh, very good. He is scrumptious." She looked delighted, and her tiny nose crinkled delightfully. God, she was seductive and enticing even when she didn't try.

"Fate doesn't always make bad choices for us, it would seem," I replied. "Shall we go in?"

We all went into the house, introductions were made to those that hadn't met yet, and then we got down to business. For all of my moaning about my relationship stress and that moment of fear when I thought Aleric and I might be parted, I hadn't really let myself think about poor Mary. A demon had taken control of her father's body, and now he wanted to marry her. Yeah, the eww-factor was at sky-high levels, and my sympathy for what she must be going through was even higher. We had to set her free, somehow.

I slung my bag down on a counter and went over to where the others were already gathered around a table. Willow went around and dropped drinks off to everyone, and I sat down to listen.

"Edana, will Adony be any help to us?" Aleric asked as Henry started to take notes.

"Who's Adony?" Henry asked, and looked at me.

"Um, he's my boss. My mentor, really. Have you ever heard of a group called Shinar?" I looked around at everyone. I knew Sabrina had, she'd visited me in my capacity as an investigator.

Everybody else shook their heads.

"We're a covert, shadow agency that operates in this world and a few others. We have been around since the dawn of time and the magicals crawled out the swamp that man oozed from. We investigate like a government agency might, but we don't report to any human agencies. We don't report to anyone really. If there are problems and we're asked to deal with them, we do. Most of the time, we only investigate our magical world when anomalies show up or when we're asked to by others."

I kept myself from glancing at Sabrina for that last part.

"I asked her to investigate the disappearance of vampires from our world," Sabrina volunteered on her own with a smile in my direction. "What did you find out?"

I glanced at Aleric, and felt terrible for a moment. He nodded at me, and I knew he trusted me and that what I had to report was important.

"Godwin seems to have them in the basement of the castle."

"Right."

She took that rather well, I thought, but I saw the glint of anger in her dark eyes. "Is there a way into your world that will allow us to go undetected?"

She turned to Aleric, and I felt pride at the gesture. He didn't think he was a leader, at all, but Sabrina's gesture told us all that he was.

"There are a few tunnels that we can get into. We have to fly to the border of our worlds, enter the caves, and then we can get into my world," Aleric told her, his face certain. He stroked at his chin, and spoke again. "The question is, what do we do when we get there?"

"How desperate will this Dagon be to stay in that body, Edana? Will he be able to live another just as easily?"

"He will, and Adony warned me about that. He told me he'd call me if he found anything out that might help us actually defeat a... demon."

I knew they were real, but I'd never seen one. I didn't know how to handle it.

"Right, then." Sabrina looked around the table at a sea of faces that stared back up at us both. "Suggestions?"

I don't know how, but Sabrina, Aleric, and I had somehow become the leaders here, but that didn't mean we wouldn't take advice from the others. They were just as important.

I saw Damesha pat Jacqui's hand and the two women nodded at each other. "I think we can come up with a binding spell. That will only keep him from leaving the body he's in, though."

"Not sure that will work," I said softly, my finger tapping at my upper lip as I thought. "If we could trap him in the body, that will ensure our safety from him taking over any of us, but will that be enough to overtake him?"

"Doubtful," Sabrina added. "He's a demon, we need to somehow destroy him. Work on the binding spell that will keep him in the body, as you suggested, but we also need to obliterate him, and any traces of him. Edana, let me know if Adony comes up with anything."

"Of course." Now the roles had switched yet again, and Sabrina was solely in charge. The men stayed at the table, happy to let us deal with most of it, for now. This was going to be a fight of wits and creativeness. Killing a demon wasn't simple, you know?

"I suggest food, and then we draw up a battle plan, in

case Adony doesn't come through." Aleric, even more exhausted now after yet another flight, said quietly from his place beside me. "I have a feeling this isn't going to happen quickly. No matter how I wish it would."

Poor Mary was still stuck in that tower. We hoped. For all we knew, Godwin might have forced the marriage already. "It all seems ridiculous."

"What do you mean?" Aleric asked.

I settled at the table as Willow started digging through her freezer for meal ideas. "Even if he's not really Godwin, the genes will still be Godwin's right? Having children with her would be disastrous."

"It's unthinkable, all of it is. We can't let it get that far. This demon must be stopped." His right hand dug through his hair, left it in a wild mess, but he was too tired to smooth it back down. "He really does want to destroy the world."

"That's usually the ultimate goal for demons, although why they always want to rule over a destroyed world, I've never quite understood. And why force something like that on Mary?"

"I think it's shock factor," Malcolm piped up. We all turned to look at him. "He's declaring that he's as powerful as the pharaohs. That he is a divine god, and therefore a divine human, by marrying his own daughter. Everybody will be so shocked in our world, and in other worlds that they'll discount him. He's insane, right?"

"Ah, I see," Henry said, and my eyes went to him. "If they all think he's an insane little despot, they'll ignore him and leave him to destroy his own world in peace. They won't pay attention to the chaos he's already causing in all of the other worlds."

"Exactly," Malcolm answered. "We have to get this done and over with. We can't let him get anywhere near Mary, first of all. Secondly, we can't let him do this to the worlds. Any of them."

We all agreed and they began to discuss logistics. The men were preparing battle plans, but Malcolm said he thought the armies in his own world would lay down their arms if they knew the princes were on the other side of the field. "My father's expulsion of both myself and Henry has caused a huge amount of discontent."

He paused, grimaced over the word father, but then continued. "I don't think they'll fight for too long, not when getting rid of Godwin solves the problem."

He didn't say father that time, I noted, but didn't judge him. He was right, Godwin was no longer his father.

"I need to sleep. I won't be any good if I don't. I've been awake for days, I've had three major flights in that time. I have to sleep, I'm sorry."

"Wait for me!" I called as Willow led him to an empty

guest room. I didn't want him to leave just yet, and that was odd for me, but I'd stopped caring about what I used to be like.

"I'm so glad you're with me," he said as he settled on the bed, and I let his head rest against my abdomen. I brushed at his hair for a few minutes, and then I pushed him back.

"Let me take this off." I unbuttoned his shirt and pulled the belts from his pants. I didn't feel like a servant as I did this, I felt like a woman taking care of the person she cared most about in the world. I let my love show through my actions, and took off his boots, and then pulled the covers over him. I leaned down, let my lips linger against his forehead, and turned the light off. He deserved to sleep for just a little while. I had no idea what had happened since I saw him last, only sketchy details, but nothing that could paint a full picture of what he'd seen. He could sleep for now. He'd need his strength, I had no doubt of that.

16

Everything settled down after Aleric went to bed. There wasn't anything we could do tonight, and Aleric was exhausted. Not just tired, but exhausted. I could see it in the way the skin hung on his face, as if the muscles were too tired to hold it up properly. And he'd been so pale beneath his tanned skin. He needed rest and I dared anyone to interrupt it.

"I have my people working on an answer," Sabrina said as I sat down. "Have you heard back from Adony yet?"

"Nothing." I sighed and sat down in a chair.

"I hope you all like spaghetti. It's about all I can produce for all of us at the moment."

"Oh, I'll pop into town and get something else if we need it." That came from Cade Alexander. I looked at him more closely. He was the oldest of the bunch, and handsome, but he didn't hold a candle to Aleric. He looked like a serious man with his business suit and perfectly cut hair, but when he looked at his wife, Jacqui, the hard edge in his eyes disappeared.

"We have enough," Willow shot back. "I always have salad on hand, and I'm going to pop some garlic bread in the oven in a minute."

"Awesome," I said and smiled. "I love that stuff, even if it doesn't love me."

"Garlic bread?" Willow asked with a pleasant smile.

"Yeah, it's up there on my list of things I can't live without."

"I don't blame you. It's on mine too."

I smiled back, and I knew there was sadness in my eyes when her left eyebrow crinkled down in confusion. I gave a gentle nod and she interpreted that to mean it was alright. And it was. I'd talk to her later.

We all pitched in to help set the table and finish off the food preparations, then I went to check on Aleric. He slept, though it wasn't peacefully. He'd thrown the covers off and had tossed around in the bed until the sheets were all over and his body was sideways. My poor love. I put a cool palm against his warm forehead. Sleep fevers weren't nice, I knew, and to have one now must be terrible.

I closed my eyes and sent him peace, or tried to. Before long his labored snores settled down and his breathing evened out. I pulled the covers back over him and soothed his hair down. I took a deep breath and left the room, my eyes troubled as I pushed my own long hair behind my ears.

I'd started to leave it down from its normal bun when Aleric and I first became real mates. He loved it down and it was only when I was doing something that I didn't want to get hair on, or when I was at work that I'd put it up from now on.

I went back to the table and sat down to sip at my wine. Bowls were being passed around, and the table went quiet as we all began to eat. I could only guess that the rest of the group had the same thoughts as me. What were we going to do? How could we save Mary? How could we sit here and eat while she was still captive?

Logic was the answer to that last one. The only thing we could do until we had some kind of plan was to keep busy. We'd eat, we'd make some kind of plans, and we'd wait, until some decision was made. The dark red wine slipped into my veins happily, and I started to feel warm as the plates were emptied and moved away.

"I'll help with the dishes," I volunteered as Willow and Henry stood up to clear the table. "You go check on the babies."

I wasn't surprised when Allana and Jadrian came to help me clear the mess we'd all made. Jadrian was the adopted brother, if I remembered correctly. The one that had developed the vampire blood problem. The one that had been made a shifter. I studied him, a handsome man, and saw that he truly cared about his red-headed mate. He touched her softly at every opportunity, and they smiled secret smiles often as they both brought dishes to the black marble counter at the side of the sink.

I stayed out of the way as they worked together to get rid of the messy dishes. I cleared trash, and took the bag out to the locked bin outside. Henry would carry that off later, but for now, the locks protected the garbage from wild bears and raccoons. It was a habit in these parts, otherwise, you'd end up with trash all over your yard.

"How are you, Edana?"

"I'm alright," I said automatically. Willow startled me, stood in the doorway like she was.

"Something's up with you and it's not just Aleric. Spill." She made a gimme motion with her fingers and I smiled at my little sister.

"You sure you want to know?" I crossed my arms under my breasts and wished I'd brought a heavier jacket. My black trousers, black turtleneck, and the black wool peacoat didn't stand up to the cold chill on the wind.

"Of course, what's up? Why are you so on edge?" She scrutinized me, her right shoulder against the door jamb before she stood up straight. "You're fine around everybody else, but with me you're on edge. Why?"

"Willow..." I started and she squinted. "Fine, grab some more wine and meet me in the living room."

This conversation had to take place some time. Now was as good as any.

She came in and we sat down on her plush, dark brown velvety soft couch. The kind of couch I swore I'd buy myself as soon as this was all over.

"So, spill."

"Do you know who your father is?" It was the best approach I could think of. Just ask.

"Mom said he was a fella she met after her sister died. That he just drifted off after a while. I never did know his name. I asked Mom about him once, and I can remember how hurt she looked. Like I'd just stabbed her in the heart with a kitchen knife."

"I can imagine." Oh this wasn't going to be easy, but I've always been a tear the Band-Aid off and get it over with kind of girl. "We have the same father."

Willow blinked for a minute, her brows knitted together, words forming on her lips, but her lungs didn't push the air through to make sound. Not for a minute anyway. "What?"

"We have the same father. After my mother died, your mother and my father started a relationship."

"I don't understand," she sputtered, her hand at her cheek as if to stroke away the confusion. "Your dad disappeared long before I was born."

"No, they just told us that so we wouldn't know." I wanted to explain more, but I barely knew more than that.

"We're sisters?" She didn't look so stunned now, and her lips actually twitched with a slight smile. "I have a sister?"

"Half sisters, but yes, sisters."

"Wow. I wonder why it was kept such a secret? Wouldn't it have been better if Mom had taken you in? I have so many questions." She poured wine into both of the glasses she'd brought and handed me one.

"Dad said…" I started but she interrupted.

"Wait, you've spoken with him?" She looked a little more upset about that. "He's alive? Why didn't he contact me?"

"Yeah, that's the part that's bothered me. I can live with him dumping me, but the fact that he hasn't contacted you pisses me off." I gulped the wine and knew there'd be another angry conversation in my future when I saw him next. "He made some excuse, said maybe they were ashamed and that's why we weren't told. I wasn't that old when you came along, old enough to know he'd gone, but not old enough to realize what had happened. I didn't know, I want you to know that."

As usual, it was all coming out a jumbled mess, but when do these conversations ever make sense? It's only later, when everything is out finally, and you can piece it all together that it finally makes some kind of sense.

"So, what's he like?" There was a gleam of excitement in her eyes, one that I couldn't allow to take root in her thoughts. She didn't deserve to build him up, just to be disappointed.

"He's scruffy, doesn't look exactly healthy. He's everything you'd expect of a man that dumped two children. Like he spends more time chasing down the bottom of a bottle than he does in the shower or at a doctor's office." I paused, let that sink in, then made sure I'd nailed that coffin shut. "He's like that guy that's run everybody out of his life, but still complains about not having any friends or how lonely he is. How he has nobody to count on, through no fault but his own."

"Oh." Disappointment made her shoulders sink, and I felt bad about that, but I couldn't keep it up. She deserved to know the truth. "So, we were better off without him?"

"No doubt." I nodded in agreement.

"He doesn't sound like the kind of man I'd want

around my child anyway. Marya will have real men in her life, men that make an effort to be in her life, she doesn't need someone like him."

"You make a good point." I didn't know if I'd ever want children, they weren't something I wanted at this point in my life, but I wasn't about to judge anybody for having them. It just wasn't a goal I had ever wanted to achieve. "He told me something, something I didn't believe at the time."

I'd totally forgotten about it when he left, so angry that he'd tracked me down and invaded my life that I'd dismissed everything but his whining about he'd had a hard life. A real hard life. As if I'd ever feel bad for him.

"What did he say?" Willow asked. I hadn't said anything for quite a while as anger flooded my blood with adrenaline.

"He said that he'd been a part of a faction of dragons in Aleric's world that tried to overthrow the king. He'd left when things got too hot, and he suspected there was more to the uprising than he was being told. He was only a minor dragon, so he wasn't exactly sure what was happening, he was just told he'd have all the drink and women he wanted so he'd followed along. Blamed it on being young and dumb." I twisted my mouth in distaste.

"So our father is a dragon?" She took another sip of wine and then looked at me. I couldn't see the dragon in her at all, only the slayer. Maybe that's why she'd had so many problems controlling her slayer, why she'd almost killed more than once. Her slayer soul must have been in turmoil.

For me, it wasn't so bad. I was more dragon than slayer, I barely felt a prickle of that side of me when I was around dragons, but Willow had really struggled.

"Yes. We're both half dragon."

"That means Marya is more dragon than slayer." She didn't look as if she knew whether to be happy or unhappy about that.

"It does, indeed. She's something unique. When she grows up that girl could be very, very special."

"Wow. This is all so…" Her hand waved in the air, she was lost for words.

"Fucked up?" I supplied with a huge grin.

"More than a little." She took another gulp of wine. "This might even be more fucked up than Godwin, Dagon, whatever, trying to marry Mary."

"That even made my head spin." I laughed, trying to ease the tension.

"What are we going to do?" She looked helpless, and I could understand, but I was optimistic. Adony would come through, somehow.

"We're going to kick demon ass," I finally said, and laughed at the ludicrous way it sounded. "It just gets worse."

"Let's hope that's as bad as it gets." Willow's words were almost a whisper.

"I'm sorry, I don't mean to be so cavalier. I don't have children of my own to think of. This must be terrifying for you." I took her hand and squeezed it gently.

"It's not so bad, I guess. Marya used to talk to me, before she was born. It was like she was this very old soul, but because she hadn't been born yet, the soul hadn't been reborn and cleansed, she was very wise. I can't hear her now, not like I used to, but I know somewhere, that wisdom still exists in her. She'll survive if something happens to me, but I'd hate to not see her grow up."

Her voice caught in a throat and I squeezed her hand again.

"Willow, look at me, girl." I hadn't called her a girl since we'd reconnected. It was something I'd done when we were all younger. It seemed the right time to do it now.

She swiped at her eyes and looked at me with a smile that wobbled. "Yes?"

"I won't let anything happen to you. I promise you that. I will not allow it." I could feel the fierce fire of my dragon come to life and blaze in my eyes. She saw it too, and her eyes went wide. "I will not have it."

"Thank you, Edana." She leaned over and wrapped

arms that were still far too delicate around my neck. "I couldn't ask for a better sister than you."

"I haven't always been great at it, but I promise, from now on, I will never stop being there for you ever again."

"I'll be right here for you too." She nestled her chin along my shoulder, and even though I wasn't a feels kind of person, I decided it felt good to have her warmth against me like that. It was... comforting. I hadn't had a lot of that in my life. As this could be my final days, it seemed right to have it now.

17

*I* was awake when dawn broke over the mountains, my mind too busy to sleep for long. Aleric began to stir beside me and I reached for him beneath the covers. He took me in his arms, naked against his chest, and we just sat there, taking comfort from each other.

It was nice to have that moment, nice to have him there with me. I'd never wanted that from a man, until Aleric. Now, I only wanted it from him. I tilted my head, dotted kisses along his jaw, and gave a soft laugh when he pulled away.

"Ticklish this morning?" I asked.

"No, I just didn't want you to prickle those soft lips with my beard stubble." He kissed me softly, and then pulled away to get out of bed. His muscular body was covered in bruises, bruises he hadn't explained but I knew meant he'd hard a difficult time with his escape from that other world.

"Was it bad?" I asked, and he stopped on the side of the bed.

"It was... difficult, but not too bad. I fell down a set of stairs when a horde of dragons came at me and all of them decided to attack me at once. Luckily, I'm a dragon and the fall wasn't too bad." He reached for a set of clothes, clothes that Willow had washed and dried last night, and put them on. "I guess we need to get ready, don't we?"

"We do." I grabbed a set Willow had given me last night and put on the blue denim pants and the red sweater she'd given me. "Is it cold in your world right now?"

"Not too bad, your sweater will be enough." He had on his boots by the time he spoke and stood up. "Let's see if we can find some food and what the others are up to."

I went to him, slid my arms around his waist and looked up at him. "I'm glad you made it back."

"I love you, Edana. It's more than just the mating bond we have, I actually love you. You're odd, you like to be alone, and you can't stand too much noise around you, but you cope. You make do, and you keep going, even when others would stop. I had to get back to you, just to see what else you'd do with your life. That, and I just can't stand to not be around you."

"Now, that's romance. My kind of romance, at least. The honest kind." I laughed softly again, not sure who was awake yet, and leaned my head into his chest. "I love you too. It wasn't something I wanted or planned for, but I have it, and I never want to be without you either."

He kissed me softly, and we said the romantic words that neither of us seemed to be able to come up with at the moment, with that kiss. He was a poet, but he knew my mind would respond to that, so he spoke to me with his body. That I could totally understand.

We pulled apart after a moment, a moment where it felt as if my heart would swell so much with love that it would burst. I thought there might have been tears in my eyes. I blinked to clear the blur, and a drop fell against my cheek.

"We can do this, Edana. We can win this fight. Don't doubt it, my warrior queen."

I gave a watery smile, and we left the room, hand in hand, to face what the day had to bring us.

Henry was up, a stack of pancakes on the counter beside where he stood at the stove top. "I've got these ready, and some bacon on this other plate here. There's juice in the fridge. Help yourselves."

"Thanks, brother." Aleric patted Henry's shoulder and I headed for the coffee pot.

We were both sat the table, juice, coffee, and plates full when the rest of our group came in. The others had on their clothes from the night before, and I don't think there was a speck of makeup on any of us. Sabrina and Jacob were absent, but they weren't really the sunlight kind of people. Vampires. Whatever.

"Are we going to have to wait until nightfall?" I asked as I noted the two empty chairs.

"More than likely," Cade Alexander broke in, his natural role as leader of his clan on display. "That will give us time to wait for a response from Adony or one of Sabrina's aides. If nothing has come by then, I guess we'll wing it, so to speak."

I studied the shifter. What would it be like to be able to shift into any animal you wanted? I glanced at Jadrian, at the end of the table. Why had he chosen a duck when he flew here, I wondered? I knew they could fly long distances, but still. A duck?

I shook off my curiosity and went about the task of eating in silence. Aleric's foot nudged up next to mine and I felt the comfort of his presence. This group was almost too much for me, too much noise, too many people, but with him there, I didn't have to pretend to be comfortable and nonchalant as I normally did. I just was because I knew he was with me.

Tension built amongst us all as the day wore on and the light began to fade. Shadows appeared in corners and we still had no answer from Adony. When Sabrina and Jacob appeared, dressed in the same clothes as the night before, but still fresh looking, we decided it was time to go ahead. Sabrina took the lead, with Jacob happy to watch from the kitchen table.

"We have two options. We wait for something else to happen, or we strike now. I can call in my vampires, and Cade can get his shifters to this cave you've spoken of, Aleric." She paused but then continued, her gaze directly on him. "Do you think your king's army will fight us?"

Very diplomatic to use the word king instead of father, I noted.

"Probably, but once they realize it's us, I doubt many will remain on that side. I think most will come to our side. Discontent is growing in that world. Not every-body is happy with the way things have changed."

"Good. Let's prepare then. Ladies, you'll be just as instrumental as the men. How are your powers?"

"I can control mine much better now," Willow volun-teered happily.

"She can too. I saw her zap a mosquito the other night," Henry added, in support of his wife.

"Since we fought the Mungon, I haven't used mine, but I have worked on control and intensity," Jacqui said.

We all turned to Damesha. "I'm mainly clairvoyant. I can hold off a few baddies, though. Don't worry about me."

"Right." Sabrina began to pace, her focus on something inward. After a moment, she stopped pacing and turned back to us. "My vampires are on the move. I say we head out."

Everybody agreed, and we all began to gather what we wanted to take. I had my bag and my phone, and went outside to wait for the others. Aleric joined me soon enough. "The Alexander women are traveling with Jacob. We'll be leaving shortly."

"Alright." I smiled at him. "Why are you looking at me like that?"

"You haven't been afraid to fly with me since we left the island. Are the heights not bothering you anymore?"

"No, I guess they aren't." I hadn't really thought about it, but he was right. I barely even batted an eyelid now when he shifted and I climbed aboard. "Something, isn't it?"

"No, it's just love. Ready?"

Everybody came outside then, and for a few minutes it was all shifting, climbing, and then flying as we all took to the now dark sky.

I wasn't ready for this, I didn't do battles. I skulked in the shadows, I picked up information, I made reports. I didn't even have a gun! What did I think I was doing?

*"You'll do fine, my dearest one. Stop your panic. It won't do you any good."* Aleric's voice, calm and reassuring, came into my mind.

*"Yeah, but, shouldn't we do some training or something?"* I sent back.

*"My brothers and I have been training our whole lives. As for the rest of you, there isn't much training you can do. Practice on the skills you have, and that's about it."*

I didn't respond. I didn't exactly have any powers. Not really. What would be my role in this?

I chewed at my lip as we traveled on, and eventually spread out on Aleric's back. I tried to find Adony with my mind, but he wasn't to be found. He must not have discovered anything. He wouldn't answer me until he had something I could use. I knew that from past experience.

I can't say that I calmed down, but I became calmer, even as Aleric started to descend. I sat up and saw that there was a line behind us, more dragons, an eagle, and raven, and... a duck far back in the distance, but still doing his best to keep up. That poor fellow. Why hadn't he chosen something faster?

We all made it to the ground, and I saw a cave opening a few feet away. I was glad I'd charged my phone, I could use it as a flashlight if nothing else. Jacqui and Willow both made my phone obsolete when they created pink orbs that gave off a bright pink light. The orbs followed them, so they went into the caves first, their men at their sides.

Sabrina's vampires showed up, along with a flock of

birds of a hundred varieties, that all came down at once. The place soon filled up with men and women as they shifted into their human shapes and followed the line that disappeared into the cave of the mouth.

There wasn't a lot said, apologies for bumping into each other, exclamations as some of the vampires created light orbs of their own in a variety of shades, but for the most part, we were all quiet as we followed Henry and Willow through the cave. We walked for half an hour, the floor gradually taking us further down before we began to climb back up. I couldn't see a portal of any kind, but when we got to the top, I saw that those in front of me had disappeared.

I hesitated and Aleric squeezed my hand. I moved forward and passed through what felt like warm energy, nothing more, no cold wet oozy feeling, just a warm pressure that felt like it was full of static, and then we were in his world.

The moon hid behind a bank of clouds, and rain fell softly on trees that had yet to shed their leaves. I wished I'd worn a raincoat, but it was too late now.

"Now what?" I asked. I felt as if this was too soon, too unplanned, crazy even without some kind of secret weapon. I knew time was running out for Mary, but now that we were here, I had to wonder if we hadn't been too hasty. We should have done more planning, we should have waited longer, this was a bad idea.

Tension crawled up the sides of my neck and make my throat tight. I could feel the way my breathing had quickened and Aleric squeezed my hand again.

"All will be well." His words were a whisper against my now wet hair in the darkness.

Some badass I was. Now that the time had come, I was afraid.

"It's normal to feel fear, Edana. You've never been in a battle before. It will keep you safe if you don't let it control you."

"Thank you." I knew he was right, and breathed deep and long.

"Where is the castle?" Sabrina asked, her voice quiet in the darkness. All of the orbs had gone out as their owner walked through the invisible border between our worlds. It was pitch black and I could barely see anything but the glow of lights in the distance.

"Down there, with the lights." Aleric pointed to the dots in the distance. "We have to go down the hill, and then up that next one."

"Right. How do you want to do this?" Sabrina spoke to the brothers as they circled her.

"Let me go down and talk to the men..." Malcolm started to say, but Aleric stopped him.

"No, we can't risk losing anybody before we even begin. I say we go down, en-masse. Make our demands known, and if they refuse, we fight." He paused, swiped at his stubble-covered jaw, and looked at his brothers. "We need to keep the element of surprise on our side. We take the armies in, wait until Godwin's men are distracted, and then we make for the towers. We keep the women with us, and we all move once the battle is on."

"Sounds solid," Sabrina spoke up and nodded in agreement. "Let's go then. No point in wasting such total darkness."

Somehow, we moved silently through the woods, despite there being hundreds of men and women behind us. Henry and Willow led the way until we made it to the open gates. Once we were at the gates, Malcolm came forward and made our demands known. "We are here for Mary. And the ashes of Dagon, the demon that inhabits my father's body."

Silence was the only answer.

18

Silence greeted Malcolm's words, and then it got ugly.

Men came screaming out of the darkness, swords raised, and shields in hand. Willow and Jacqui responded first: wide bolts of pink light—followed by a rainbow of vampire fire—flew at the rushing men, but only a few were hit. Enough broke through that we were hit by a wall of screaming men and metal.

We fell back, and the rushing army of shifters followed.

Thousands of people fought in the darkness that soon flared into flames of many colors, and vampires fought shifters and witches fought whoever attacked them. Slayers, now mated, controlled the powers they had, Arista and Willow both, but mine was only a puny light that did little more than keep Aleric from direct contact with anyone.

We fought, noise and smoke filled the air, and then it went quiet. Some of the other men had realized that it was the Dragon Prince brothers who headed this invading army and started to put down their arms. Others continued to fight until they either died or real-ized they were outnumbered. A group of twenty ran back through the gates and closed them before we could cross into the castle proper.

"Now what?" Sabrina called out of the darkness.

"Here, come here," Aleric called out. Once the people had gathered, he began to speak again. "Well then, they know we're here."

I re-positioned my bag on my shoulder and realized that I, stupidly, still had it on me. I felt the box inside bump against my hip and thought about that paper again. Would that somehow work better in this world? It had come from my world, but was it meant to be read here?

Fire-tipped arrows began to fly from overhead, and we all ducked, but Aleric screamed as burning pitch and metal lodged in his right shoulder.

"Aleric!" I screamed his name and dragged him down beneath me as more arrows flew. Someone dragged us both out of harm's way, behind a wagon, and I franti-cally searched for a way to treat him.

"Don't do this, don't do this." I wasn't sure what I meant, but I'm fairly certain I meant don't die. The flames had gone out, but the metal arrow was still lodged in his shoulder.

"He's passed out from the pain. Let me." Sabrina came to me just as Willow came up behind her and produced a small orb, small enough for us to see his wound, but not so much we'd become a target again. "We can deal with this. Men, carry him to the back."

Two men carried Aleric to the back of our lines and disappeared into the darkness.

"I have to go with him."

"No, you have to stay here with us," Sabrina said sharply. "You have a role in this, I just haven't figured out what it is yet."

I glared at her and wanted to argue, but all I could do back there was get in the way. Up here, I might be able to do something. Then the box bumped my hip again.

"Do you think…? Here." I took out the box from my bag and handed it to Sabrina. It wouldn't open of course so I took it back.

The box opened once I'd placed it in my palm and I took the scroll out. The ends came apart, and for the first time, the images were calm and made sense. The words started to make sense to me too, even if they were in a dragon language. I studied it, but Sabrina's curiosity got the better of her.

"What is it?"

"A dragon scroll of some kind, that's what Aleric told me it was. We found it in a remote cabin in our world. I don't know what it is exactly. I've had it for a while, there are images, but they were always moving around, I could never make sense of them."

"A dragon scroll? That might be just what we need." Sabrina didn't reach for it, she just looked at it.

"It only seems to work for me. Willow!" I whispered loudly into the darkness. "Willow, I need you!"

"I'm here." My sister came to me, followed by Arista and her husband.

"Hold this, see if you can tell what it says."

"No. It's just moving around all weird, trippy." Willow handed it to Arista, whose eyes wobbled around the same way before she handed it back to me.

"Neither of you see the image on it?"

"No, it's just weird symbols that keep moving around," Arista said.

"Fine. It's for me then." Damnit. I wanted to go to Aleric. I knew there wasn't much I could do, the medics in the back of our lines would have to do their best because if anything happened to him, I'd go crazy.

I could still feel him as if he was with me, so I knew he wasn't in bad shape, but that could change. He had a flaming arrow stuck in his shoulder, for fuck's sake!

"Well, what does it tell you?" Sabrina finally asked, and I looked at the scroll.

"For the dragon that cannot dragon," it said in a rather cheeky kind of way. Imagine, for the dragon that can't dragon. This really was for me. It even had my sarcasm!

"Dragon that cannot dragon?" Willow asked, her face scrunched up.

"I can't shift," I revealed. "I should be able to, but I can't. I just kind of end up in a pile on the floor."

"What?" Arista asked, her face just as confused as Willows.

"It's hard to explain. Willow and I are sisters, did she tell you?" I hadn't even thought to inform anybody else. It had been our business, but now I thought it needed to be explained a little more.

"No! What the fuck?" Arista's eyes were wide. "How did that happen?"

"I'll explain later. Suffice it to say, we're half-dragons. In Willow's case, she's more slayer than dragon. I'm more dragon."

"Oh."

"The problem is, I should be able to shift, but can't." I looked down at the map and mumbled the rest. "Something's always held me back."

"Oh." This time it was Willow that spoke.

"So what use is the scroll for a dragon that can't

dragon?" Sabrina asked. There was no sidetracking her, I could tell.

"I don't know yet." I watched the images shift around in a way that reminded me of my brain at the moment. An image of a door, the momentary flicker of a woman being dragged from a cell, a roaring dragon unlike any I'd seen before. What did it all mean?

I put it away, safe in my bag, just as a roar came from the gates and a new wave came at us. Only this time, the men came in their animal forms. Bears and wolves charged at us. A sword appeared in my hand, placed there by somebody, and I did my best to wield the unfamiliar weapon as a wolf jumped straight for my throat.

I screamed a sound of rage and fear as I sliced and felt metal crush through bone. The wolf fell, but a bear replaced it, and then another, and they fell but more kept coming. Where did they all come from? I barely had time to think, much less look for anyone else, so I kept hacking and stabbing, and I knew I'd have nightmares about the way a sword sinks into soft flesh and hits bone for years.

A wolf came at me from behind and I heard a loud explosion just as I felt gore splatter my back. I didn't stop, I couldn't, because another wolf came at me, teeth bared and eyes full of hate. "Just fuck off, won't you? Fuck me, I'm exhausted!"

The wolf snarled, pounced, and I brought the slim

blade up to swipe it away. The blade was so sharp the wolf's head flew from its body. I'd backed up a good distance by then. We weren't winning, but we weren't exactly losing either. Far more of the wolves and bears were dead than our side. I saw that some of the wolves and bears that had joined us were locked in battle with their brethren in the moment I had to breathe before a bear fighting with a mountain lion knocked me over as it charged at the large cat. A tiger jumped on the back of the bear and I knew it was someone from the Alexander clan.

I tumbled away, and then stood up, sword still in my hand. I was not, let me repeat not, any kind of superhero in that moment, but I looked around, waiting for my next opponent. I was exhausted, and at some point during this battle, I'd become aware that Aleric had faded from me, just a little, but enough to notice. What was happening with him?

I chopped at another wolf and wondered just how many were in that castle. I ran after that one fell, and found my way to the hastily erected tents where the wounded were being treated by a witch shifter from Allana's clan. I could hear the Louisiana swamp all but dripping from her sultry voice as she directed young men and women to patients.

"This 'uns losing a lotta blood. Somebody bring me some of that curdling powder."

"What the fuck is curdling powder?" I asked and found that the patient she was talking about was Aleric.

"It's meant to clot the blood, mon cher." Only, when she said mon cher, it sounded like "mon sha".

"What's wrong with him?"

"Well, he took an arrow to his shoulder, cher, what you expect?" She was beautiful, but in that second I wanted to slap her.

"No shit. I meant, why isn't his blood clotting?" Don't make me go all dragon on you now, lady, you're far too beautiful for me to fuck your face up, I'm fairly certain my glare said, because she sniffed a little, pursed her lips, and finally answered my question.

"I would guess the arrow's tip was coated in something to keep the blood from clotting. That or it nicked a vein. Either way, my powder will stop that."

Only, it didn't, and instead of the blood stopping, Aleric jerked and more blood shot out of the wound. We were all covered in the hot spray of it as he jerked on the floor, surrounded by several others in the barely lit tent.

"Oh my God, fix him!" I screamed and somebody pulled me away from the tent. Only, that wasn't good enough for me. I barged right back in and put my hands over his wound. Like that could stop the geyser coming out of his back! Blood seeped from between my fingers, and the woman treating him pushed me away.

"Move if you don't want him to die!" She pushed a

pad of gauze on the wound and barked orders. "One of you idiots gave me the wrong powder. Find it! NOW!"

She roared the words and glanced at me, fear in her eyes. I could feel the dragon stirring within me as the life ebbed away from Aleric.

"Get out. Now." She hissed the words, but something was happening in my head. I couldn't hear her, I read the words on her lips as something twitched in my head. Something... snapped.

Maybe I was in shock, I wondered as I backed out of the tent. Maybe the weeks of tension, and then worry, and now the blood and the gore, the killing, and Aleric's life just... exploding away in a violent rain of gore, had finally broken my mind. I was in the darkness, but staring back into the tent as the woman did...stuff to Aleric's wound. She ran a line into his arm while I watched, something in my head just gone. I couldn't think, I could only *see*. I couldn't speak, I could only *feel*.

*Pain.*

I felt pain grip me, pain unlike anything I've ever felt before as things within me tore, broke, came *apart!* My God, I'm dying, was my final thought before the world imploded into one point of light. Only a tiny fraction that grew smaller then blinked out.

Then, the world exploded in noise and color, and I was high in the sky. Only, I wasn't me. I turned my head and saw metallic, silver wings. Below me, I saw a pair of dragon claws, needle-sharp points at the end of each toe. And within me fire built, hot and scorching. It built until I opened my mouth and spewed it out. Straight down at the wolves and bears that still fought for the demon that would be king of us all.

They scattered below me, and somewhere in my reptilian brain, I wondered why the dragon princes hadn't done this already. I flew, flames still pouring from my mouth, as the beasts below me ran. I noticed when the other dragons shifted and joined me at last. Jacob, Malcolm, and Henry were in the air with me, and we had the castle surrounded. The walls started to crumble under the heat of so much damaging fire and the rage started to ebb away.

I didn't think as a human, but I wasn't wholly animal either. I knew what I needed to do and I flew to the tower where Mary was kept. I didn't know it, but the moon gleamed off of my metallic, but still leathery skin, a strange combination, but one that kept me safe, I knew. I shrank in size as I came near the bars of Mary's cell, her form apparent to me through the stone walls. Dragon eyes can see through walls much better than mechanical heat detectors can.

She was chained to a bed, silver shackles clasped around her wrists, thin strips of fur in place to protect her dragon skin from the metal that could burn her. I took a look at my skin, wondered if it was really silver and if this made me immune, and decided not to chance it. I directed a small flame at the metal, one that she couldn't produce while she was chained like that, and gave a little hop when the shackles opened and released her.

"Who are you?" she asked and looked into my eyes. I was less than six inches tall at the point, but she saw my eyes and knew me for who I was. "Edana?"

I gave another hop, and she quickly shifted into a size that matched mine. Together, we flew out of the tower, and out into the night. I had Mary, but there was still a demon to deal with. And my own death, if the fact that I no longer felt Aleric was any indication of what had happened. Pain twisted my guts. I wanted to fall to the ground and burn into ash, to join him, but knew my work wasn't done. Not yet. As an agent of Shinar, I had research to do. As a dragon, I had aid to give. As a sister, I had to make sure my sister lived through this before I could let go of my life. The screams would have to come later. For now, I had a demon to destroy. I gripped my bag tightly in my claws and flew down to the entrance to the castle proper. It was time to take this fucker out.

19

I flew down to the ground, to the area where I sensed my sister stood, and shifted out of my dragon shape. Instead of the pain I expected, I just felt something akin to a pop, and then I was human once more.

"Thank God y'all somehow go back to wearing clothes when you do that," Willow said as she looked at me with a smirk. Then Mary came down and shifted, and Henry and Malcolm came to join us.

The battles had stopped, but I didn't want to give them time to regroup. Sabrina might have been leading this fight to begin with, but it was my turn now.

"Right, this is what we're going to do." I didn't pause to ask about Aleric, I still couldn't feel him, and as long as I didn't think about it too much, I knew we could get through this. Somehow. "Ladies, you're going to go to that gate and blast any son of a bitch that tries to move. Henry, Mary, Malcolm? Shift and follow me."

I was a little bit surprised when they did as I instructed, but I thought it was more that it looked like I had an idea of what I was doing that made them pay attention. I was going on gut instinct at the moment, and nothing more.

We all took up our positions and forms, and the dragons followed me into the sky.

"Follow me down." I could smell the demon, I could almost sense him as I drew down into the courtyard of the castle. Hidden behind a window on the upper floor that overlooked the courtyard, the beast that would destroy us all waited to find out his fate.

I wasn't in the mood to be generous.

"Dagon!" I called out as I landed and shifted into a human once more.

Godwin's body, shriveled and old now, but still a reflection of his sons', turned to me. "Ah, dragon. Slayer. You call me by an old name. In the past, I have been called Abbadon. Belias. Leviathan, even. As man changed and changed their gods, I went from a god in my own right to little more than a demon. My name was forgotten, except for some rather obscure texts, but now I hear it once more."

"Not for long." The other dragons came in and the witches came, too. With their ability to harness energy and the dragon's ability to harness fire, we could keep Dagon caged. I hoped.

I dug in my bag, not willing to talk anymore with the demon, but he wouldn't shut up. I pulled out the box, and waited for him to finish. I felt vibrations, small and gentle, in the palm of my hand, as the box seemed to register that whatever that scroll was, it was needed now.

"For centuries I have roamed this world. I came with the elders, those creatures that perplex you so. We came to this planet when it was little more than poisonous steam and molten rock that bubbled and quaked as it gave birth to itself. When the earth cooled, and the first humans came, we were there to guide them, to offer our assistance as they began the journey that brought us to this moment. Thousands of years have passed, millions, and I have seen man go from little more than a grubby little hobbit, to well, this." He waved his arms about. "I created the vampires when I became bored with the religious idolatry, and the werewolves when the Byzantines were plotting out which leader to kill next, which everyday activity would now be declared a sin."

"Are you about finished?" I asked, my eyes glued to where he stood, dressed in white stockings, a long fur coat, and a rather jaunty beret.

"Oh, do give me a minute, princess. I suspect whatever is in that box will be the end of me." His fingers waggled in the direction of my hand before he clasped his hands behind his back.

"You and your Shinar have wanted to know your origins for a long time now, and here I am telling you what they are. You think that would get me a few more moments of life." His white eyebrow, thick and almost caterpillar-like, winged over his eye before he turned away to twist his equally thick mustache. "The dragons, the fairies, they were all the work of the fairies. The bears, the vampires, the wolves, those are all my children, my gift to the world. A gift it seems that I have destroyed."

He wandered back to the window, still within our reach in the wide hall made of uncovered limestone. The floor was even made of the uneven rocks, but it had stood for hundreds of years over the courtyard, nobody could fault the craftsmanship. Godwin stood at the window, one arm against the frame, the other behind his back. "I do have to admit, I went a little mad in those years when the world had forgotten my name, but when the first temples were found, when the sand was swept away and fingers stroked the symbol for my name, I came back to the world. I awoke, angry, hungry for more power, for more people to know my name."

"So you're pissed off because centuries later the fish came to be a symbol for Christianity and not for you?"

I'd learned that about him when I did a little research the night before.

"Oh, that old man and his inability to understand that language. God of the fishes, indeed. No, I was just a different life-form, an alien if you will, that helped the people to harvest their crops and sometimes had the power to make their childbearing years more fruitful. But in the darkness, I went mad. I've done terrible things, horrible things, and maybe I'm still just a little bit mad. I would crush you if I could, dragon, but I know when the jig is up."

The box opened then, and the scroll unfurled. "Here demon. Meet your fate."

I don't know why I said it, it just seemed appropriate. The box fell to pieces and the scroll began to glow in my hand. Those that stood behind Godwin moved forward and he stepped away. "Just another moment."

"No. Enough is enough. You've polluted not just this world, but all of the worlds with your insanity. Time to pay for your crimes." I had no idea what was about to happen, but some force I didn't understand took over at that point.

A symbol came from the glowing paper, a golden shimmery light that moved, grew, until it completely engulfed Godwin's form and Dagon's soul. The demon screamed, protested, tried to fight, but in the end, the light blinded us all and we had to look away. The light began to draw in after that, until the room was all but dark except for the light from the row of torches. The paper rested in the middle of us all, but it wasn't done yet.

The pieces of the box drew towards the paper, and so did all of us. I felt my dragon come awake, and I shifted, not against my will, but it wasn't something I wanted to do. I saw the others shift and the witches draw close. Once we were close enough, we all blasted the paper with fire, with energy, until even the ashes were totally obliterated. This was the end of Dagon. This was the end of the taint that had polluted our world. I expected birds to chirp overhead, or the sky to lighten and angels to sing our praises, and they might have, but I didn't know it because I passed out.

"SHE'S FINE, stop hovering over her."

I knew that voice, I thought, as the world came back in a jumble of noise and sore muscles. I wanted to go back to where it was warm, and soft, and dark, and most of all quiet. I clenched my hand around whatever softness rested beneath my head and tried to tune the noise and voices out.

"She isn't fine, she hasn't woke up yet!"

Aleric's voice? Was that his voice? But why was it coming from beneath my head?

I stirred, murmured, but didn't open my eyes.

"You see now, you've woken her up! You don't know what she's been through! You should have let her sleep." Willow's voice.

"Are you sure she actually shifted?" Aleric again.

"Into the most beautiful dragon I've ever seen!" Willow's voice sounded awed, as if I'd impressed her.

"Well then. I'm sorry I missed that."

"I might be able to do it again, now that I'm awake," I groused a bit as I pushed myself up. I saw that my bed had actually been my mate. "You're not dead."

"No, did you think I was? Because I thought I was for a little while there." He gave me that cheeky grin of his and I wanted to slap him and kiss him at the same time.

"I thought you were." I shuddered at the memory. "Dagon's done?"

"Oh yes, done and dusted. Nothing left to even think about coming back together to cause chaos for any of us." Willow gave me a chirpy smile and I realized then we weren't in tents, but in a very fancy room. "Oh."

"Oh yes. Castle baby. Palace even." She held her arms out and twirled. "Aleric's been declared the king, this could be your new home."

"What? Wait! How long was I out?" I looked around and saw light coming from a window.

"Just a day," Aleric said softly as he stood up to join me at the window. Outside I saw rolling green hills, golden sunshine, and workers busy clearing debris from the battles.

"What happened? What did I miss?"

"Not a lot. Malcolm and Henry have decided to stay in your world with their wives. I have been made the king. That is, if you want a king for a mate? If not, I can give it to Mary."

"I... whoa." The world went a little woozy and I tottered back to the bed in bare feet. I was dressed in a white cotton sleeveless nightgown that hung down to my knees. Romantic and sweet. A good choice, I thought stupidly.

"Yeah, it's a lot to take in. Do you want to be a queen, my love?"

"A queen?" I asked, again with the stupid.

"Sure, we can rule over this world, and make little princesses and princes, or we can say no and go back to your world. I would like to stay here long enough to make sure everything is stable again, that the vampires and shifters are all happy, drug-free and able to make babies, but I can leave after that."

"She may not have a choice, really." A very odd voice came from the shadows of the room then. The Elders. Those strange beings with their weirdo eyes!

"What do you mean?" I asked, not sure if I should be

snarky or not to these beings that could make me disappear with a thought.

"You won the crown, lawfully. You destroyed Godwin, not Aleric. It was that scroll that finished him, and you used it. You are the queen of this domain, if you so choose."

"Wow." I felt myself sink further into the softness of the bed. "Seriously?"

"Indeed. You are a true dragon now, blooded and vetted. You are meant for this role, Edana. You, far more than anyone else, are ready for this role."

"But babies?"

"The world will be fruitful once more, without Godwin's taint. If you don't want children of your own, you can direct that one of your nieces or nephews can be the next in line. Or adopt, there's always adoption."

"Right." Mmm, no, let's leave that decision for later, I thought. "So, I'm a queen now?"

"A badass one, if we may say so." The odd voice of the two that came out as one, masculine and feminine at the same time, held a note of mirth.

"I'm glad to have been of service." What else are you supposed to say to aliens? Elders? Whatever the hell they are?

"We shall leave you now, madam, if you don't mind. We are tired of this world lately, and need a break. It is in good hands. For now." With that, the pair blinked out the same way old televisions used to when you hit the power button.

"Well then. I guess the choice is made." I looked around at my sister and at Aleric, who were both smiling.

"Queen Edana," they said at the same time. And we all cracked up laughing. It had been hell on earth, the fear before the battle. I knew I'd have nightmares about the actual battle, and that moment that Godwin blinked out himself. But I had my mate, and my sister. All would be well now. I'd made sure of it.

20

*Five Years Later*

Marya and Galen, the best of friends, played beneath a tree in a shadowed forest, their song an ancient folk song that had been brought back to life with their mixed voices. It was a dragon saga, a song of our past, and I smiled as I watched them play.

"They're growing so fast," I said as I looked at their mothers.

"Who'd have known this would be our lives now?" Arista said, her right hand cradling her belly, her other rocking a rocker at her side. Inside, her daughter, Annalise slept peacefully.

"I wasn't expecting to have another baby so soon after Marya, I know that. And I ended up with triplets!" Willow smiled happily as she looked to where her little dark-haired sons played with their father, Henry, in the water of the stream we'd decided to have a picnic by.

"I haven't told Aleric yet," I said, my eyes alight with a secret smile, and my lips twisted in happiness. "He's going to be so pleased."

"It took you long enough to make that decision!" Arista teased, but I knew she wasn't being mean.

"I wanted to be ready. I'm not like you two, I didn't come pre-installed with an acceptance that I'd be a mother. I didn't want to have anyone that dependent on me, you know? I could barely cope with my own quirks."

"You've come a long way from that woman, Edana, and even if you hadn't, we'd still love you."

"In the end, I decided I wanted a baby because I wanted Aleric to be a father, I wanted to have the love you two have for your children. I wanted to have someone to follow in my footsteps, to take my path even further."

"Those are good reasons. Aleric is going to make one hell of a father," Willow said, happily.

"Speaking of..." I saw him coming out of the forest, to the clearing where we sat. "Hello, Thad."

"Hi there, Edana. Thanks for having me."

"I think you deserve it." I smiled at him as he sat down next to Willow and she took his hand.

Arista's parents came out of the woods too, their own golden wedding bands back where they belonged. Even Rachel, Willow's mother, came out, her hand in that of a wolf shifter she'd met here.

Everybody was paired off and happy now. My father had done the most work of all of us, when it came to character anyway. He no longer drank, he'd taken a course or ten to be helpful around the castle, and he'd become a man we could depend on to act as a father. It had taken a year of patience on his part, and frustration from Willow and I, but we'd finally given him that chance to prove himself. I'm glad we had.

"Edana, dearest, can I show you something?"

Aleric came out of the water and towards me. I took his hand and stood as he led me through the forest.

I had on a long, burgundy cape to keep the chill at bay, and sandals with golden straps. We traipsed through the forest, there were no fleas or ticks here to worry over, and he'd taken me to the deepest, darkest part of it before I knew it.

"I've never been here before," I said and looked around.

"No, it's a place that only queens can come to when they are... well, expecting."

"How did you know?"

"Did the others not tell you our children can talk to us from the moment they are conceived?" he asked with a smirk of happiness. "I've known about her longer than you have."

"The doctor only just confirmed it. What do you mean speak? She hasn't spoken to me." I felt a little hurt over that.

"She will when she has something to say. For now, you're doing a good job, so she doesn't need to tell you anything." I'd tickle that smirk right off his face if he didn't get rid of it soon.

"Oh? And what did you do that needed correcting?"

"I wasn't bringing you enough fruit. She wanted fruit."

"Is that why you've been plying me with tangerines and apples?" I laughed then, I'd wondered about that.

"Yes, she likes tangy fruit,"

"A girl then. Wow." I went to him and he pulled me to an entrance I hadn't seen earlier. It went into a cave, a cave lit with pink orbs and blue torches. "What is this?"

"The place where queen mothers come to get away from it all and to have their every need met."

"Oh my," I said.

He led me to the edge of a dark pool, lit by a white light beneath. Bubbles frothed from the surface and I smelled the most magical scent of orange blossoms and lemongrass.

"Be careful now, the rocks can be slippery." Aleric helped me to take off the dress and the sandals, before I slid into the waters. It was warm, but not too hot, just right, and as soon as I was neck deep I began to feel energy flow through me, revitalizing me.

"In the coming years, you can come here to get away from the castle, and your burdens there. You will find whatever food you desire on a tray over there." Aleric pointed and I saw a silver tray with the exact thing I wanted on it. I'd had an odd craving for vegetarian lasagna lately, and that looked delicious. "And over there, music will pipe through, or television if you prefer."

"A woman-cave, literally." Oh, this was gorgeous.

Being a queen could be tiresome, but it was the most rewarding thing I'd ever done. So far. This baby was going to top all of that I suspect. "Come here with me."

"Oh no, I'm not allowed in the waters. Those are all for you. I'll be on the bed, over here, waiting for you when you are finished."

It was an amazing place, and I loved it. I swam for a few minutes, until I felt as though I was bursting at the seams with energy. I also began to feel a deep throb of desire in my belly for Aleric. He just looked so good, on that bed all alone, his legs wrapped in leather.

"Come here," he beckoned me softly. He knew what that look in my eyes meant by now. "Stand here."

I'd left the water, soaking wet, and stood before him, naked and proud.

"Lift your leg, my sweet," he whispered, and his lips brushed at my thigh when I obeyed. Only he could give me orders, and only when I let him.

The water had already untwisted the knots of concern and anxiety that had made my shoulders and back ache. Now, Aleric's lips soothed me just a little more. His teeth nipped as he came close to my center, his right hand on my ass to hold me close. "Let me taste you, my Queen. Let me make you writhe on my tongue as pleasure turns you into a temptress."

His fingers stroked over the damp folds of my center and then moved up to my nipples. He teased each one into a tight peak as his lips brushed softly at the folds he'd only stroked over a moment ago. His other hand came down, slid between the folds, and opened me. His fingers found their way inside me as he did two other things simultaneously.

His mouth opened, hot and wet, just as his other fingers clamped down on my right nipple. I wanted him to be rough, I wanted him hard and fast, but he knew what I wanted even more than that. I wanted to scream his name.

His tongue flicked gently over my most sensitive parts, despite the way he breathed hard and fast, eager to make me come, to be inside of me. His tongue flicked at me again, just as his fingers moved inside of me, and the ones on my nipple gripped tighter, and I was off. My hips pressed me deeper into his face, and I cried out a sound that was his name, that was nothing. I didn't care, because pleasure pulsed through me.

He could do that now, make me come almost on command. It was an art he'd mastered long ago. I loved him for it.

When it was done, when the waves had stopped, he pulled me down on the bed, bent me over, and pushed his own pants away. I almost wished I still had my dress on. There was something about the way his hands would knot the material on my back as he fucked into me that always made me so... *wet.*

His thick length probed at my entrance, and I moved to take him. Slick, full, and smooth he slid into me with a groan. His hands gripped at my waist and I felt him shift behind me. He wasn't all the way in, not yet. I inhaled and blew out just as he sank that final inch into me. I couldn't stop the shudder that coursed up my spine, any more than I could stop the way I clenched around him.

We moved together, our dragons already greedy and out for their share of the pleasure to come.

"Move, Edana. Fuck me, baby." His hands gripped at my waist and I did as I was told once more.

I met each of his deep thrusts with a hard grind to

keep him inside me, to keep him in just the right spot to make it good, but make it hurt a little.

I wanted more though, my dragon wanted more, and I could hear myself growl as we moved together. A snarl that said more, give me more.

I felt every inch of Aleric as he plunged into me, over and over again. I was too greedy to wait, and I slid my hand down, to that sweet spot of madness, and flicked it with my finger.

His fingers bit into me when I clenched around him, and that little bit of pain sent me over the edge into another world. A world where my dragon came out to play as my body writhed below. Orange and blue flames reached for Aleric, beckoned him closer. I saw him there, and he came towards me with a fierce rush. "My queen."

I heard it in my head as if he was right in front of me. I pulled him to my flames until we twisted and turned into one being, then we flew even higher.

Later, he would love me soft and slow, but right now he knew this was what I'd needed. He knew me as no other man had ever known me. Not the lovers I'd brought home only to kick out when I was finished with them. Not Adony, who knew me better than most, but had been a mentor, a replacement father, not a lover. This man, this dragon, had finally understood me and what I needed the most.

It had taken me a very long time to come to terms with the fact that he was my mate, all of those years ago, and I'd refused to have a huge wedding. I was not a ballgown kind of girl. But he'd waited, he'd been patient, until he'd figured out that what he really needed to do was take me. Make me his, then I would be.

Now, we were partners, mates, in every way. He was my king and I worshiped him as much as he worshiped me. Our lives had not been a promise we could keep when we first came together, there was too much danger to make that promise. Now, babies were being born, the world had become a place of peace and prosperity, and we were still in love.

"I can't believe you haven't grown tired of me," I said as we caught our breath on the huge bed.

"The same could be said of me." He laughed. "I'm the one that still writes crappy poetry!"

"Oh, it's not crappy, Aleric!"

"You're lips are like two Twizzlers that have been licked to slick smoothness." He repeated a line from a recent effort.

"Alright, not your best work, I'll give you that, but 'your eyes are two crystals that see the soul of the world and reflect it with silver clarity' was pretty damned fine." I kissed his shoulder playfully.

"I think only you think so, my love." He peeked out

from under the arm over his eyes and then hid again, but he was smiling.

"Our daughter will like your poetry." My hand went to my stomach, and I felt that inner peace she'd brought to me.

"She'll have to. She may be the only one who reads it after a while." He chuckled and pulled me close. "I'll have to stop showing it to you, my pride can't take many more of those snorts."

"You wrote 'your fingers pluck the essence of bad smells from the air and replace them with only scents that delight', Aleric. It was funny." I tickled his ribs and he laughed.

"You're right. That was atrocious."

"It was." I rested my head on his shoulder and looked into his eyes. "You know I love your bad poetry even more than I love Shelley or Yeats, right?"

"I should hope so. They're old and dead. Totally unoriginal, that dying thing they did. Real artists would have found a way to live and grow in their art."

"Let's hope you do some growing soon then." I ran from the bed after that one, snatched up my dress and sandals, and ran from the cave. "We have to get back to our picnic!"

Aleric chased me and we both laughed as we ran, until he caught me and pressed me up against a tree.

"I will never have enough of you, will I?"

"No, the mating will make sure of that." I smiled happily, my eyes on his in the darkness. I'd put my dress back on as I ran, but my shoes were still in my hands so I could clench him closer. I did the next best thing and held my mouth up for his kiss. "Tell me you love me, Aleric."

"I love you, Edana. I have from the moment I met you. It wasn't just the mating that drew me to you, it was you. That sharp defiance, those beautiful eyes, and these amazing tits. My god, your tits get more amazing every day!" He filled his hands with the globes in question and smothered his face in my cleavage.

"Really?" I said with exasperation but a pleased smile. The man did love my boobs.

"Oh yes, really. But, I love your smile, your really odd sense of humor, and the fact that you saved us all from Godwin is a big one too."

I sobered when he mentioned the man who used to be his father. "I wish we could get your father back for you."

"He left my life a long time ago. I know that now, even if I had forgotten. It's done. We have a new life now, and we have only the future to look forward to." He kissed the tip of my nose just as my niece and her cousin came to join us in our fairy tale moment.

"Come play with us. Show us the dragons again, please!"

One day, this little girl may very well be queen herself in her own world, I thought, as the niece who had me wrapped around her finger took my hand. But that was a matter for the future. Right now, I had a family to love, and that vegetarian lasagna to eat. Life was perfect.

# ABOUT THE AUTHOR

Selina Coffey is a romance writer who lives happily in London with her husband and son. She is a hopeless romantic who grew up always believing in love and she is not ashamed to admit this! It is this belief that makes her so passionate about writing crazy love stories.

A stereotypical girly girl, she loves shopping. So whenever she gets a chance and the spare cash, you will probably find her browsing online for the next pair of shoes to add to her collection.!

You can find her online at
www.selinacoffey.com

Contact her at
hello@selinacoffey.com